cat
brushing

cat brushing

and other stories

jane campbell

Grove Press
New York

First published in 2022 in Great Britain by riverrun, an imprint of Quercus Editions Limited.

First Grove Atlantic hardcover edition: August 2022

Published simultaneously in Canada
Printed in the United States of America

Typeset by CC Book Production

Library of Congress Cataloging-in-Publication data is available for this title.

ISBN 978-0-8021-6002-7
eISBN 978-0-8021-6003-4

Grove Press
an imprint of Grove Atlantic
154 West 14th Street
New York, NY 10011

Distributed by Publishers Group West

groveatlantic.com

22 23 24 25 26   10 9 8 7 6 5 4 3 2 1

For my mother
whose own story was never told

CONTENTS

SUSAN AND MIFFY

THE LUST OF AN OLD MAN is disgusting but the lust of an old woman is worse. Everyone knows that. Certainly, Susan knew it.

Susan was a woman who had never put a foot over the line. Susan, though indisputably plain, had landed a handsome, solvent husband. Susan had grunted and gasped her way through thirty years of marital congress, as she assumed all women did, for really, what was the point of sex? Susan had conceived her children without difficulty and delivered them promptly. Susan, who had loved them in the same efficient and slightly distant manner in which

3

she herself had been loved, was known to be lucky for there had never been any big problems in her life.

She was always called Susan, never Sue or Susie, for there was something about her that called for a formal regard; she was slightly aloof, as though apart from ordinary mortal mess. Susan sat in her bed in the hospital wing of the geriatric unit with her hair combed and a paperback (high on the list of bestselling novels) open in her clean hands and, two weeks after her eighty-sixth birthday, looked at the young woman who was reaching up to change a light bulb and felt lust stirring within her withered loins.

That last statement is not only an unforgivable cliché but is also not strictly true. Lust as everyone knows has many different forms and when something is completely new to us we have yet to learn to recognise it. What happened to Susan was that she felt tears spring into her eyes and her heart began to thud in an unfamiliar way. It is because I am old, she told herself, for whenever she had been able to find a reason for something she felt better. Maybe I am dying, she said to herself, and reflected as usual that death would solve a number of problems.

However, even as she dismissed her feelings her eyes were drawn back to Miffy's long golden arms which were as smooth and shiny as syrup as they reached upwards towards the light fitting and she watched Miffy's long golden hair slide further down her back as she struggled to get the bulb into place and then her eyes moved over Miffy's body as it wiggled and jiggled with the effort of her task; over her breasts, over her waist, over her stomach and down to her thighs as she thought, So that is what youth is.

And she could see how utterly beautiful a young body can be, how shapely, how proportionate, how cleverly curved, how lithe and graceful and just miraculous. And she began to wonder if it was possible that, once, she had had that look? And tangled up with these thoughts was another new and very troubling feeling: Susan longed to touch Miffy. Touch everything. She wanted to reach out and move her hands over the young woman's breasts and around her back and into the curve of her waist and out over the curve of her hips and around to the curve of her . . . and here Susan had to stop. And then she was filled with shame, with a deep, deep shame handed down to her by the many years of British middle-class Protestant womanhood that had preceded her own upbringing. Susan knew it was important to be, above all, ladylike. It was not proper, it was never proper, to think in certain ways, to dress or eat or drink or speak in certain ways. And fantasies such as these were outrageously, dreadfully wrong. They were plain wrong, she told herself. They were disgusting. And Susan moved her eyes away from Miffy, who had anyway by now managed to get the bulb in place, and she again focused her eyes on the pages of her insipid book.

It has to be said, that, because she had, in a sense, never been used, Susan was far better-looking in her old age than in her youth. There was about her the rather cold virtue of undamaged porcelain; as though she had been locked away in a cabinet behind a glass door and it would have been true to say that, in many ways, she had never been touched. She was a small woman with well-cut hair and, in a useful metaphor for her life, since she had always worn rubber gloves for all her household tasks, her hands were still young hands with delicate fingers and smooth pink nails.

It was these hands as they held the book that caught Miffy's eye as she reassembled herself, pulling her uniform back into shape and laughing at the effort she had had to make. And then she saw the bedside table with its glass of water, its decanter, its comb, all neatly laid out; she saw the dreadful book and the tired and anxious face that bent above it and then she looked again at the hands as though recognising that this husk of a person had once been a delicate and lovely woman.

It was as though she were standing beside a bonfire of some sort and a small ember shot upwards, fell through the air and burst into light within her heart and sparked with its heat a glow of compassion.

She moved over to Susan's bed, making those immemorial gestures of care and concern, patting pillows, smoothing sheets, tucking in blankets, batting away from the covers anything that might harm or inconvenience the occupant of the bed. And as she did this she said, 'How are you today, Mrs Stallworthy?'

Susan, who was an inheritor of and believer in hierarchies and who did not believe in associating with the staff, found herself compelled to say, 'Very well, thank you, Miffy. You had quite a struggle with that light bulb, didn't you?'

She looked at Miffy's hand, resting on the coarse weave of the washed-out hospital blanket, and remembered that once upon a time, as a treat, at tea-time, she would be allowed hot-buttered toast with Lyle's Golden Syrup and as the butter dripped off the warm toast beneath the sheen of the liquid syrup it was exactly that colour; the colour of Miffy's skin. And Susan had to stop herself reaching out to touch it and almost, she thought, confusedly, from putting it to her mouth.

She lowered her eyes in case Miffy saw the desire in them but Miffy was laughing now.

'Oh, you wouldn't believe it. We were told we had to get a bloke from maintenance to do it but if we had waited for him it would have been weeks. And we have to have our light, don't we, Mrs Stallworthy?' Then, glancing at the name card above Susan's bed, she added, 'Or may I call you, Susan?'

Miffy's voice was soft and lilting, emphasising the

second syllable. Susan loved the sound of her own name in Miffy's mouth.

'I call you Miffy,' she smiled. And thus it turned out that the bonfire was real and well and truly lit and so the two women were now at risk from the flames. That was not, however, clear at the start. All that Miffy thought as she left was what a sweet, sad person Susan was and how much she wanted to be able to console and look after her. Meanwhile Susan was looking at the tea tray that had been put in front of her, trying to remember what it was like to be sitting there looking at it before this encounter with Miffy; for Susan had an analytical mind and she could tell that something irreversible had occurred. If she had known it was love she would have been surprised; if she had been told that it was lust she would have been horrified. Fortunately, lust continued to conceal itself beneath an urgent longing to see Miffy again, accompanied by a faint and wistful hope that next time she might be allowed to touch her hand. Being a naturally secretive person, or perhaps a private person would be a better description, she was accustomed to saying nothing of how she felt; however, like all lovers who have stumbled upon the glory of their emotions for the first time she was also bursting with the knowledge and longing to share it.

The following day Stephen came to visit his mother. Stephen was a careful man. He worked as an economist in Geneva for the UN. He could say little about his work but he was by nature quite like his mother so that suited him too. He was married to Cynthia who was an unremarkable but kind wife.

'Poor thing,' she had said quite reasonably, 'She needs visitors. There will be nothing else to cheer her up.'

Susan had never paid much attention to the reasons for her incarceration in what she thought of as the Care Home. She knew it was sensible that she should be there and that the place had been carefully chosen by her sons. During the preceding months she had had a couple of falls and there had been a suspicion of a small stroke. Tests confirmed it.

Nor had she ever paid much attention to her body other than to keep it clean and appropriately clothed. Now she looked at it with dismay. She saw how the furrowed skin hung in dry folds from her arms and how the skin on her thighs was churned into scaly patches. On her stomach were thin layers of pallid flesh where she had lost ten pounds after the first fall. Although the initial speculation was a little TIA as the doctors called it, she had lost weight without meaning to and so the c word was mentioned. Once she had thought it would be a relief to shed this unrewarding shell but now, since it was the only medium through which she could contact Miffy, she did not want to lose it. Concern and revulsion mingled in an unhappy combination. Thinking of asking Miffy if she could hold her hand made her feel suddenly ashamed of this misshapen ugly body. Such are the perils of love and lust; better to feel nothing, but it was too late for Susan. The fire had been lit.

She wondered if she could communicate some of this to Stephen who, undoubtedly, loved and cared for her. Stephen, unaware of the tumult of his mother's emotions, looked kindly at her.

'How are you, Mum? Things OK around here? Are they looking after you?'

'Yes, indeed. There are some very nice members of staff.'

'You getting to know them?' He was surprised.

'There's a young woman on work experience . . .'

'I hope they are properly trained? I don't want just anyone nursing you, Mum.'

'Oh no, she is finding out what the job entails. Talks to the old people . . .' Susan's voice trailed away.

'Let me know if she becomes too familiar; I don't want anyone stepping out of line.'

'How ill am I, Stephen?'

'Don't you worry about that. You just focus on getting better.'

Susan stared at him from behind the barriers that lay between them; the years of indifferent affection and the undemanding conversations that swerved away from intimacy or distress. He patted her hand.

'I'll let Mickey know you would like to see him. He's good at knowing this kind of stuff.' Mickey was the younger son and a lawyer.

In many ways, although she had never really defined it

like this, Mickey was her favourite. He too had been reared in her diffident fashion but when Gerald had got angry with her, it was Mickey who had said, 'Oh come off it, Dad. That's just Mum. You know she doesn't mean any harm.'

Had she not meant harm?

It was so difficult to know.

Meanwhile, as Susan was struggling with these new sensations, Miffy was enjoying her familiar ones. She was naked and sitting cross-legged on the bed watching her boyfriend in the shower. She was damp with love and desire and was holding her head back and running her hands through her tangled hair just because it felt so good to do so as her fingers scraped against her scalp and her hair bounced onto her shoulders. She was so pulsing with energy and imminent passion that her eyes were shining and her skin was glowing.

'Hurry up,' she said, but Ant did not hear her through the pouring water.

In part her surge of pity for Susan had arisen from the superfluity of sensual delights her current life offered her. She would have been as responsive to a lost kitten or an abandoned puppy: she felt full, full of good things, full of happy sweet things; she felt she was overflowing with good fortune and luck and happiness and when she saw the small sad woman cowering in her tidy bed beside her tidy bedside table she had wanted to scoop her up and cuddle her. She had tried to explain something of this to Ant who had said, 'Yuck, Miffy. How can you want to touch them? They are so old; they smell disgusting.'

'No worse than you,' she had laughed, pushing him away, 'Go and have a shower.'

Sometimes the gods are kind and resolve our desires with an extraordinary and abundant generosity. When Miffy returned the following afternoon she brought with her a toilet bag full of what she described as 'my goodies'. She sat on the bed and took Susan's left hand in her own gentle hands and stroked it thoughtfully; turning it over to examine the palm as though she would peer into Susan's soul. Then she sighed and took out a nail file and began to shape Susan's fingernails, saying, 'You really have the loveliest hands, Susan.'

She softened the cuticles and tidied up the nails, as she said, 'You really do not have much that needs doing.' She massaged an aromatic cream into Susan's hand and then wiped and painted the nails a brilliant scarlet. 'What do you think, Susan? You should show them off. You have lovely long nailbeds.'

Then Miffy took the other hand and started on that.

Susan looked at the top of Miffy's head; at the narrow parting from which the blonde hair fell in what she wanted to describe as sheaves of gold. She is made of gold, she said to herself, and wondered if she were beginning to dement. She laid her painted hand on the white sheets and thought it looked wildly exotic and fascinating. When Miffy left she gave Susan the hand cream. 'I love the scent, don't you?' Susan went to sleep clutching it in her hand.

The following day Mickey came to visit. Susan looked at Mickey's cheerful face.

'I've brought us a treat, Mum.' He took two small tumblers and a half quart bottle from his knapsack. The whisky burnt her throat and she had never really liked the taste but she loved the air of conspiracy that this introduced between them.

'Mickey, the strangest thing has happened.'

'What, in here?' and he looked around with a comical air of disbelief.

She wanted to say, 'I think I've fallen in love,' but the words died in her throat. She took another sip.

'I've met someone.'

Mickey looked at his mother and saw nothing but the weary old face, its features worn out as though already partially erased by time. He dreaded her dying but it would in some ways simplify life. He and Abby were not getting on, there was a girl in the office, but he did not want to open that particular can of worms.

'Who have you met then?'

The unbridgeable distance lay between them. She feared mockery. She feared disbelief. But more than anything she feared his disgust.

'One of the nurses. She used to work at Pauline's. You know. The hairdresser.' How easily and smoothly these words fell off her tongue. Where did she learn to dissemble so efficiently? Living with Gerald, of course. Never letting how she felt show. Or almost never.

'That's nice. Another drop?'

She accepted it. She would always accept anything Mickey had to offer and be grateful.

Susan's new room was one of the best in the ward. After their visits, her sons had insisted that she needed a private room. It was on the corner of the building with wide windows in two walls and it got the afternoon sun. Each afternoon Susan would watch the square of sunlight move across the floor and wonder when Miffy would step into it again. She found that her mind was full of Miffy and she had formed a list of questions she wanted to ask her. The most important was always, 'When will I see you again?' but she was afraid of seeming too demanding. She diligently rubbed the cream into her hands, separating the fingers as Miffy had done and massaging between them.

The following morning when the doctor was doing his rounds Susan was not sitting up as neatly and tidily as usual. He requested some tests. Mickey was away from home on a conference for a few days but Stephen picked up the call in Geneva and said he would be over as soon as possible.

Susan's face had collapsed on one side. Stephen looked at her with alarm.

'You may be a great-grandmother soon, Mum.'

Susan would never have taken much pleasure in this. She had never been very fond of babies. She was glad of course that her sons were sensibly married to reliable wives and had stable families. The fact that the grandchildren were now starting to reproduce was admirable in many ways, however she could not quite see how that would concern her.

'That's nice,' she said.

'Julia is expecting a baby next year. We hope you'll be up and about by then.'

Susan's heart was squeezed by fear. Surely she would not have to go home? Suddenly, like watching a sunrise, she saw through the partly open door a slim golden shape.

'Miffy!'

Stephen, who was sitting in the armchair, turned his head and saw a young woman who was hesitating in the doorway.

'I'm afraid we're busy,' he said.

Miffy vanished. From Susan's eyes fell great tears.

'She is my life,' she said to Stephen who noted this as being an aspect of the disturbing behaviour that he had been warned his mother might start to exhibit.

When Stephen had left, Miffy came back into the room and sat on the side of the bed. She looked at Susan's wet face.

'I think I am dying, Miffy. No-one will tell me.'

'Are you afraid of dying?'

'I wasn't until I met you. Now I am. Miffy, I signed something. I can't remember what it says. I don't know what they are going to do.'

'I will find out,' said Miffy. And she leant forward and patted Susan's face with a tissue as she promised that she would come to see her the following day and bring the information.

Twenty-four hours later and Susan was sitting up in bed watching the sunlight that was sweeping into the room. It was a soft, primrose-coloured light; flattering every surface, gentling the corners of the angular hospital furniture.

Meanwhile Miffy, normally quite a law-abiding person, was opening the filing cabinet she was not allowed to open in the office which she was forbidden to enter. Knowing that she would see Miffy soon was for Susan both a joy and a burden; the waiting was terrible.

Miffy was a little breathless, more from anxiety than any exertion, when she ran along the corridor to the room. 'I think it says, Susan, I am so sorry, but I think it says that you do not want to be resuscitated. It has your signature, like you said.'

Susan could remember the conversations with Gerald and herself as her sons held out the living will for her to sign. How readily we decide to dispense with a life when there is nothing left to use it for, she thought.

'Don't cry,' Miffy said to Susan, 'I'm sure they don't bother to read them.'

She sat on the edge of the bed and the sunlight wrapped her in gold as she took Susan's hand. 'How are your nails doing? Still OK?'

'I have so many questions,' said Susan, 'Why are you called Miffy?'

'My name is Myfanwy. My family is Welsh.'

'I think your skin is like syrup.'

As Miffy was laughing, Susan ran her hands with their beautiful nails down the sides of Miffy's face across her cheekbones, around her mouth and into the contours of her neck and then she spread her fingers over Miffy's shoulders beneath the uniform. Her fingertips seemed to have grown an extra layer of sensation; it was as if she could read through them. She shut her eyes and felt the small pulse in the indentation of Miffy's collarbone. It seemed to her that she had never before known what life was.

'Don't be afraid,' said Miffy. 'I don't want you to be afraid. Do you believe in God?'

'When I look at you, Miffy, I . . . yes . . . I believe in God.'

Miffy looked at Susan's face, ardent with longing, and then, in turn, as an infant mimics its mother, she placed her hands on either side of Susan's face and drew it towards her own. She pressed her lips against Susan's and then, as she drew back, she saw an expression in Susan's eyes which meant that she again pressed her lips against Susan's and parted her lips so her tongue could slide between Susan's parched lips. A shiver ran through Susan. A silver sliver of a shiver. A shimmering glissando of joy.

'Miffy, I love you. Please don't leave me.'

Smiling, Miffy placed her hands gently on Susan's shoulders. 'What do you think? Should we run away together?'

'I could afford to keep us,' said Susan.

'And I could look after you,' said Miffy.

And they stared into each other's eyes, knowing that they neither could nor would escape their respective fates: for they were not, of course, the first star-crossed dreamers to be defeated by affection, duty and habit. Nor would they be the last.

'Will you come back tomorrow, Miffy?'

'I promise. I promise I will see you tomorrow.'

That evening as the sunlight withdrew leaving her room full of the mystical undertones of twilight Susan lay there bathed in bliss. Slowly as the gentle light faded a full moon appeared banding the room with silver. Susan held her hands up in the ghostly light. She admired her beautiful pale hands: she watched them twisting and twining, plaiting the streams of light; so her mind ran on, playing with images, poetry, dreams. Plaiting the moonbeams. I must tell Miffy, she thought. I will say, 'I was plaiting the moonbeams,' and she could see Miffy smile as though she were still sitting beside her. Full of remembered moments with her loved one, confident of the loved one's return, she was suspended in a between world of bliss; radiant, weightless, happy. She had never known such a feeling of peace. Feeling therefore happy and peaceful she also felt very, very sleepy. She gave her hands with their long scarlet nailbeds one final appreciative glance and then turned onto her left side and placing one scented hand under her left cheek she curled up her legs into the shape she was in in her mother's womb. In her right hand she held the empty tube of hand cream. Tomorrow Miffy would bring her a new one. She fell asleep and slept deeply with a smile on her lips.

At the end of the night shift the alarm was raised by the duty nurse. It appeared that Susan had experienced a massive cardiac event during the night and had died in her sleep. How

fortunate she had been, everyone said, and would repeat endlessly over the next few days. How lucky Susan had been. We
should all be so lucky as to die as swiftly and simply as that.

By 2 p.m. all trace of Susan had been removed from the
room and when Miffy ran along the corridor she stopped
in the doorway and then sat down quickly on the edge of
the empty bed, gulping, trying to breathe for it seemed as
though her chest was being squashed and her head might
explode. When she had regained control she walked along
to the office where they told her that Susan had died in the
night. She was very lucky, they said. She didn't suffer. It
was time for her to go.

'Did you . . .' Miffy started to ask but she knew she
would not get an answer so she walked out into the car
park where she stood for a long time trying to remember
why she was there. After a while she moved to the bus stop
and caught the bus home where she tried to explain to Ant
why she was crying. Why she could not stop crying. Ant,
who was a primary school teacher and would therefore have
known a lot about empathy, listened patiently to her story.

'Old people die,' he said, between her sobs, for to him old people were just a bunch of aliens.

'They die, Miffy. Often it is a blessed relief to them. And to their families.'

And then later in her story, 'I can't believe that Miffy. That is just gross. So gross. What were you thinking of? That's not exactly in your job description. Come on, Miffy. Please stop crying.'

Eventually, Miffy realised she was alone with this experience.

'They die, Miffy. She had had a good long life! She had a family. You said her sons looked after her. She was a very lucky old woman.'

Miffy wept and wept.

'You didn't fucking kiss her? An old woman like that?'

Once again Miffy found herself gulping for air as though under water.

The following day she went back to the geriatric unit to say that she had recognised that this work was not for her and she would not be coming in any more. She was warned that abandoning your work experience commitment like that did not look good on a young person's CV; she would find it hard to get another placement. Miffy said she didn't care. She walked down the corridor and in the sun-filled room she saw a stranger in Susan's bed. She walked home instead of taking the bus and as she walked a dry wind sprang up and whisked an annoying strand of hair into her eyes.

'I will get it cut tomorrow,' she said to herself.

Meanwhile, the sons had been told that their mother had suffered a sudden cardiac arrest. It was likely she had not been in pain. There were no signs of distress and she had not rung the bell which was well within reach; she had not called out or indicated that she needed help in any way. She was found lying on her side with an empty tube of hand cream clutched in her right hand, the only unusual feature. The staff on night duty had assiduously checked her throughout the night. She had, of course, had the usual medication. Her sons expressed relief at their mother's lack of suffering and together fulfilled all the necessary requirements for a cremation. An inoffensive humanist ceremony preceded it and the sons and the clusters of their families were all there as well as some remote cousins people mostly forgot about.

What a pity, they all said, that she did not live long enough to see her first great-grandchild. It would have given her something to live for. What a shame. It would have made her so happy. If only she had seen Julia's baby. She would have enjoyed that, poor dear. But how fortunate she was to go like that. Really, how lucky. We should all be so lucky.

After the ceremony, the brothers collected the urn containing her ashes and Stephen placed it next to Gerald's. Mickey looked at the urn anxiously but Stephen said, 'Oh, come on. He can't hurt her now.'

As they walked back to the car Mickey said, 'We did do everything we could for her, didn't we?'

'Of course we did,' said Stephen.

THE SCRATCH

IT WAS A SMALL SCRATCH, really quite insignificant, not even painful, which was the weird thing, because it was bleeding quite a lot and Nell could not recall how she had done it. It was on the top of the lower joint of the forefinger on her left hand. The hand she used less. She had spent some time trying to think what on earth she could have done to damage herself in this way. What drawers had she opened carelessly, perhaps, knives rearranged, had she handled scissors? It was not there this morning, that she was quite sure of. And she had put the washing out on the line and she would have noticed it then. It was deep too.

The edges serrated and purpling as they began to show the bruising they must have experienced. What had she done? It was all a bit concerning. Was she really forgetting things? There was that phone call yesterday to her son-in-law, about their upcoming visit. The airline strike was being publicised, she had skimmed it in the morning paper and then when he had answered the phone she was quite put out. It was her daughter she had hoped to speak to. She had recovered herself enough to make polite conversation, well that was the plan, but she had ended up gabbling something about would the strike affect his visit until he patiently, or maybe not so patiently, now she thought about it, explained that that was the week past. Of course it was. Of course it absolutely was. And she was so careful these days to put everything, but everything in her diary. How had she mistaken a midnight that had passed for a midnight that was to come? She felt cross with herself; mortified would be more honest. And just because she had expected her daughter to pick up. And her daughter would have been more understanding, although the understanding was always tinged with a sense that if only her mother had led a more orderly life no-one would be in the mess they were in now. Maybe that was unfair, though. Maybe it was just her own bad conscience. They do say that as you get older your defences begin to weaken. The old barriers behind which she could once shelter, with humour, with panache, even, certainly, at times, with a degree of courage, well, they all tumble down as the years pass. Just as running upstairs becomes a lost art and skipping down them becomes impossible, so the capacity to forget is lost. There is the persecution of remembering. Remembering so much. Those midnight hours, dark nights of the soul, where remorse bites hard and the past presses against you. And she could not forget that this was almost certainly, although of course, they had never talked about it, what her mother had felt as she grew older. The unrelenting comparison at that time between her active mind and her mother's slow one. Her preoccupations versus her mother's. Why had she been so cruel, no there was no other word for it, why was she so cruel towards her mother at the end? Admittedly it was mainly at a distance, those insuperable distances of miles and countries as well as of those others of interests and upbringing. Why did it

all seem so impossible? Why had she not known that it is
not help you need but just to have someone on your side?
Someone on your side; right or wrong, through thick and
thin, all that stuff. Just someone who did not judge, just
accepted. Who did not diagnose a silly lapse like mixing
up the Sunday midnights, who did not judge the wearing
of wrong clothes, the extra drink, the unwise friendship, if
that is what it was. Trying so hard to keep a grip on reality
seemed like a waste of time when after all reality was so
cruel. That face in the mirror in the morning, the ghastly
hair, the lost waistline. Some, of course, are slim. Some, of
course, don't drink or eat too much. But what else was left?
The scratch was glazing over now, beginning to form a scab.
That is what she needed. A scab over all the wounds. But
she could not remember how she had done it.

It was the following morning that she noticed the cut on
her leg. Her right leg, just above her ankle. Of course,
with age her skin had become so friable: it bled easily and
the blood thinners didn't help. However, she really could
not remember how she had done this. Easily done though.

Knocking against the corner of a chair; that vegetable basket in the kitchen was a bit of a liability. She examined the cut after her morning bath. She had washed it well and now she dried it and stuck on some Elastoplast. Not like the old stuff; that would stay on for days. She remembered the agony of pulling it off a hairy arm or leg. In those days, hair grew everywhere; now it was only on her face. Only two days until they arrived. She felt so embarrassed about that mix-up with the airline strike. So stupid. And if she was covered with bits of Elastoplast of course they would assume the worst.

The next day she found a slit on the skin of her inner thigh. This was really a puzzle. Such soft skin she had there. She could remember Basil resting his head there, kissing it. 'The best bit of you,' he would say.

'That's not very flattering,' she would protest, laughing at him. 'And me with all these moisturisers on my face,' but he would persist in his lovely gentle way.

'It is the best bit of you, Nell, the softest skin. And only I see it. That makes it mine.' The cut was about three inches long and not terribly deep. Of course, it could be dangerous just there. There were arteries and veins and things like that. And it would be really dangerous to cut into those. She could have bled to death. At least her son-in-law wouldn't see this cut. It was difficult putting the plaster on it. She had to sit in the most undignified way; legs splayed, probing about, trying to see what the hell she was doing. But it would have made Basil laugh to see her. They would have laughed together. Those were good times.

And it was that night that she had the dream. Or was it a memory? She really couldn't be sure. She decided that dream was more probable but she knew it was also a memory. It was in her mind when she woke up. It had happened a long time ago. She and Basil, not long married, were on a package tour to Melbourne. A sort of late honeymoon. He had cousins there, silly people. It was hot, hot and the hotel was large, modern, with big patio doors in all the rooms. The sort that let the heat in. Along the whole of that wall were long red curtains in a sort of open-weave net-like material. She and Basil were on the top floor. Very grand. They had been down by the pool and she had decided to go back up to the room to get a book, was it, or sun-cream?

Something indispensable, obviously. She had pulled a shirt on over her bikini and slipped on some flip-flops and caught the lift up. She was walking along the corridor when she had heard the wail. It sounded desperate. A real cry for help, as she said later. So she knocked on the door and heard it again and tried the handle and it was open and she walked in. The first thing she noticed were stripes of red light, filtered through the curtains, lying on the pale carpet like patterns falling into a church through stained glass. Then she saw a young girl, very skinny, standing there naked. She had her arms held out with the fingers cupped to catch the blood from all the cuts. There was blood on her stomach as well. The strange thing was that, as Nell looked at her, from somewhere in her memory was the image of a crucifix, the white marble body against the dark wood of the cross. The drooping, dignified head, the thin agonised arms, the gaunt ribs, the crossed feet nailed like the wrists to the cross. The weight must have been carried now by the hands, now by the feet as the body, too tall for its circumscribed torture, shifted its position in its dying agony. But the position of the feet had also dislodged the symmetry of the body and

one hip had projected slightly to the side. It was the curve
of that slender hip that she remembered then, for it had
been so feminine, that line between the ribs, the stretched
abdomen and the projection of the hip bone; it was so
delicately fleshed, so smoothly sculpted that now when she
looked at the girl she saw, in the time it took her to move
another step closer to her, that same curve in her body, that
same tender sloping shape. The girl looked at Nell and Nell,
well, she could only have been about five years older, but
she felt very grown up as she walked over to the girl. She
could see the slightness of her and the sweetness of her
shape and she could smell the blood.

'Hold me. Hold me.'

Nell took another step towards her. She took the girl in
her arms and held her to her own body, feeling the pressure of the girl's small breasts on her own, the warmth of
the blood that now lay on the girl's stomach moistening
her own. She wrapped her arms around her and the girl
drooped her head against Nell's shoulder. She felt the girl's
moist palms on her back, and the girl's hips relax against her
own and Nell felt within herself an aching surge of sexual

arousal. The girl raised her head and pressed her lips to Nell's cheek. Her hair brushed against Nell's lips and Nell could smell the powerful odour of her skin, cold to the touch but damp with the heat of the oppressive air. Still holding her close, Nell moved one hand up over the girl's shoulder blade and, circling the bleeding arm with her fingers, she moved her hand slowly and carefully along to the girl's pliable wrist until she held it at eye level as delicately and as decisively as though she were waltzing with her. Nell could see that the young blood had stopped flowing and was beginning to glaze and to clot in the crevices of the flesh. She led her to one of the twin beds and laid her on it. She grabbed a towel from the bathroom and tucked it around her as the girl was shivering. Her teeth were chattering. Shock, Nell supposed. But she was also covered in perspiration so Nell assumed she might feel cold. Nell then dialled reception and said there was an emergency. It seemed like hours but they did arrive. A stretcher and someone whom Nell took to be a nurse. There was a wailing ambulance outside by now. She left her to them. The girl's eyes were closed. Nell hoped she would not die.

Basil had barely noticed Nell had been gone. She heard later that the girl did survive. Of course the whole hotel was rabbiting on about it. The girl was staying there with her parents and her sister. Apparently she had a habit of cutting herself. 'Terribly disturbed,' was everyone's verdict. 'Awful mental disorder.' How strange it was. And people discussed the rationale for it; how the endorphins rush out and you are soothed for a while, like with opioids. Of course, once it was known that Nell had found her, everyone wanted to know what she had seen, what she had done. Nell said little. The girl was sacrosanct to her. Even Basil never got the full story. Nell told him how waif-like the girl was. How lovely. But she never told him about the memory of the figure on the cross and of course she never told him about the arousal. Of course not. He was a good man and no fool. But Nell knew he wouldn't understand. Who would?

Later on Nell often wondered what it was she saw in the girl. The truth is, she used to say to herself, 'I think she was me, a version of me.' For ages after that, when she got the chance, Nell used to look at herself naked in the bathroom mirror on the back of the door. She used to hold her arms out as the girl had done and slide one hip out to mimic that seductive angle. She had realised that the crucifix that had come to mind was the one that used to hang in the convent where she was schooled. Naturally, after a while she got over all that. But the memory of that moment in the hot red light of the curtained hotel room lay like a little nugget of gold in the dust and debris of her life.

They would arrive tomorrow. Never had her mind felt so clear. Never had she been more confident of the justice of what she was doing. Her own misshapen body was distasteful to her now. She was pleased that she had finally rediscovered what she had had to forget. The loveliness of that girl, the scent of her blood, the angle of her hips, the perfume arising from her hair and her damp skin. How beautiful she had been. Nell drew the razor down over the tangled veins in her wrist as gently as a violinist draws her bow over the strings of her violin and felt the same glory. This was peace. This indeed might be heaven. The blood flowed swiftly from the old veins although old veins are difficult. All day she lay among the bloodstained rumpled sheets, wrapped in the arms of that young beautiful body from her past, utterly at peace.

Her daughter and son-in-law arrived at about tea-time as they had said they would but later than they had intended. Traffic and all that. They had brought a sponge cake. They found her in the bedroom. Her son-in-law walked straight across to the window and opened the curtains and pushed the window open. 'God, what a mess,' he said. 'What a disgusting mess. What a dreadful way to die. We should have come earlier. I knew we should.'

CAT BRUSHING

THIS MORNING I was brushing the cat as I watched the rain come across the water towards us. She is a Siamese and smooth-haired and like me quite old and her fur is not as strong or as resilient as it used to be but she arched her back with delight and raised her head so that I could reach her throat, the most vulnerable part of her. And seeing her respond like this to the strong smooth strokes I could see myself in bed with one of the lovers, and my own arching and offering, and wondered, when I had finished with the brushing, whether she felt as I had when it was over: not just brushed but glad, even grateful, to have been brushed. In other words, was it the moment only with her, or was there a reflective pleasure as well?

When I had finished she walked away while I stood up with some difficulty. She lies fully extended on the kitchen floor for the brushing process while I kneel beside her. I find these days I have to hold onto the edge of the counter to get to my feet but I tell myself it is good exercise for my thighs. And then, inevitably, the other exercises my thighs once got involved in come to mind.

The kitchen door was open and I could see the water in the Great Sound which early this morning resembled sheeted metal on which the tiny humps of the islands rested. I walked to the door and watched as the whole horizon and all the sea and the land became cloudy with the strengthening rain. The cat sat beside my feet. We both looked out. I know of course that we do not see the same thing. Her perception is different in every respect. I feel the dampness and smell it and hear the raindrops in quite a different way from her. But she sits and watches it with me with just the same degree of satisfaction. It is a tremendous view to have available all the time and I feel very lucky. The kitchen gives onto the veranda where there is a jumble of chairs and tables and a large corner sofa. The cat and I sit here for hours. The view from here is like a mobile panorama for old people since there is always some movement somewhere. There are the big regular ferries of course for the locals and the distant huge ungainly liners stuffed with tourists moored out at Dockyard but apart from these there is the constant traffic of smaller boats. Sometimes, when the sea is a pellucid blue in the sunlight a little yacht with white sails will float across the mesmerising expanse of colour and I will watch it travel from one side of the Sound to the other, wondering about the people within, loving its calm progress in the sea breezes. At night the boats turn into patterns of bright green and red and orange lights and chug back home to anchor alongside the docks of lucky home-owners.

The cat and I watch all this together. This is Bermuda. Tourist paradise. Rich home to rich financiers like my generous son. We know we are very lucky. My son is nearly fifty and his new wife is in her late thirties. Not really such an age gap. She makes him happy. At least I hope she does. The cat and I have known him for much longer, of course. Well, I have known him all his life and the cat for many years.

While we watch our view I knit because apparently it is good for old fingers while the cat does nothing but blink wisely and push her warmth against my thigh. I do wonder if she knows about loneliness, although cats are said to be uninterested in anything except their own comfort.

I love this view but of course, it is not my view. I do not own it any more than I own the cat. We are both housed and fed by my son since I am now judged too old to live alone. The cat does not know this and since I am the one who gets up first in the morning and feeds her before opening the kitchen door she may think I am her primary caretaker, if that is the phrase, and therefore her owner. And it is my bed that the cat comes to at night after hunting and she curls up under the sheets between my knees. It is strange to have her there but I believe she used to sleep with my son before he married. I will not complain; anything between my legs is welcome these days.

I own nothing now, except, I suppose, my body and my mind, such as they are after so many decades of use. Ill-use, sometimes. But at least, thank God, they have been used and I did not waste them. I cannot of course tell my son this.

He looks so fondly at the two of us when we sit together in the evening, the cat on my knee, while I watch the screen. In his head, as in the head of the world, an old woman and her cat are a charming representation of innocence.

The cat and I are learning about the process of dispossession. Ageing is often represented as an accumulation, of disease, of discomforts, of wrinkles, but it is really a process of dispossession, of rights, of respect, of desire, of all those things you once so casually owned and enjoyed. I could seduce men quite easily once, after I had escaped from my husband of course. They were married men and so I was safe with them. We could drown in mutual waves of desire and longing and yearning leading to brief ecstatic periods of gratification and delight and an enormous gratitude for the sheer good fortune of our circumstances. We found it so easy to please each other. And that too is another dispossession: the capacity to please. Once when I arched my back and let out little miaows of pleasure my lovers thrilled with the knowledge of their potency. Now, I offer a few inches of knitting to my son. It is a terrible loss.

So in the absence of being able to please I try to be

useful. And not disgusting. The cat got sick yesterday. She does sometimes. She hunts, has always hunted but is, I feel, less successful than she used to be. There it is again, the loss. She catches the slower prey and eats bits of it and it may be already ill or diseased.

It is a terrible thought but I am in a similar place, as the young people say. I saw my son's face as he mopped up the small patch of green vomit and so I know how he will look when one day I lose control and crap on my skirt and he sees a brown smudge and smells it and knows my disgrace. Dispossessed you see, of control and elegance and all the charms I had in abundance once.

We both have a bit of a weight issue. She has been put on a diet by the vet which is why she has three restricted meals a day instead of being allowed to graze as most cats are. I try to eat less but I am lumpy and shapeless now. If I went around on my hands and knees all the time (and, of course, that brings dear S to mind) I too would have a stomach that hung out towards the floor. Once it was such a provocative pose.

I have had a bit of a cough recently. Well, for several

months now, I suppose. My daughter-in-law took me to the doctor last week and he said it might be an allergy. I think that is ridiculous. When I was child no-one had allergies. These days there are peanut allergies, milk allergies, gluten allergies. I could go on. We just had food or no food. And we had pets. I said, do you mean asthma. But the doctor, young, smart, who did not seem to want to look at my saggy old breasts when he listened to my chest, so humiliating, was rather vague. He sort of winked at my daughter-in-law the way adults do when there are children around.

After we got home I said nothing hoping the subject would go away but this morning my son told me the doctor thinks I have become allergic to the cat. I said, nonsense. After all, Siamese are the least likely of all cats to cause allergies, everyone knows that. And we've been living alongside each other now for three years. But he insisted that the doctor was very confident about this diagnosis.

'The doctor said, as we become older we can develop new allergies, even to Siamese cats,' he said.

'So what will you do?' I asked. He was late for work by then so he said, we'll talk when I get home tonight. He'll be back in a few hours. I am afraid. I am afraid for myself and for the cat.

Sometimes I watch her washing herself. She licks and licks and I wonder what it feels like. I wish I could lick myself. It was P who was best at that. He loved it, would disappear down there between my legs for hours. No, of course, I exaggerate but I never knew quite why it was such fun for him. I would of course be arching and miaowing and murmuring as usual and I could please him that way as much as he pleased me. K on the other hand did nothing like that. 'The boys would say if you'll suck pussy you'll suck anything,' he used to tell me and I smiled because how ridiculous. He was so prim in some ways and so lascivious in others. But it was C who would sleep beside me, like the cat. He was my sleeper. I watch the cat curled in upon herself and think that is how we were. Like one body, one smoothly aligned set of muscles and skin.

I hate knitting in the same way I used to think I hated or at least didn't like cats. That was when I lived alone. I needed my freedom and space and no dependents. But the cat is my fellow inmate now and I think we understand each other.

She has an ageing face, as do I, of course. Her eyes are as blue and as large as ever and her ears still enchantingly bat-like, but her black nose is not a young nose and her jaw is an old jaw. The lips, if that is the word, of her mouth are uneven and discoloured. And although the fur alongside her muzzle has always been pale (she is a Blue Point) it seems to me it is whiter now. She has virtually no teeth. They are a weakness in Siamese. This must exacerbate the hunting problem. I still have my teeth but heavily veneered and crowned and so on. They hurt quite a lot. Sometimes I think it would be simpler to have them extracted as the cat's have been.

I heard my daughter-in-law mention a baby and that she believes that cats carry germs. I think of this while I stroke the cat and admire her serene profile. But I mustn't speak. I have been reprimanded for speaking too sharply to children.

Once my students were afraid of me or at least of my occasional tongue-lashings. I had a reputation for being quite a disciplinarian but it was one I cherished. I told one student off once and she never offended again and I learnt later from another member of staff that she had said afterwards, 'She was furious with me but I knew she still loved me.' And I did. And I was loved and feared in return. It was a good place to be. Now I am loved, I suppose, but also expected to be sweet and fluffy. And quiet. What a fate.

My son will be home soon. My daughter-in-law will be late in tonight. I think he will bring up the subject of the cat while she is not here and then he can say it is her concern. If they got rid of the cat where would she go? My daughter-in-law prides herself on not being sentimental about animals.

I suppose the truth is they would kill her and then I would be expected to knit for the baby.

I sometimes wonder if it is incumbent upon me to defend the cat to the death, as it were. I hesitate only because, as with all love relationships, I am not sure how much altruism is in it. After all, without the cat here there would be no more cat-brushing. I shall miss her terribly.

LAMIA

I T WAS A LATE AFTERNOON in February and Linda was
sitting once more, as she had been promising herself
she would, beside the vast watery plain of the Zambezi.
In front of her were the banks of rising spray more than a
mile wide marking the precipitous descent of the swollen
river into the abyss. The Victoria Falls. Mosi-o-tunya.
She had walked the short distance to the rainforest earlier this afternoon and was almost surprised there was no
sound of angelic trumpets as she peered once more into the
burgeoning mists and tested the dank slipperiness of the
rocks. It was, she reminded herself, a three-hundred-foot

drop. It was here that the memories lay, sweeping out of the spray into her eyes, making them water so that she blinked against the images in her mind. For her this was a sacred place, holy and enchanted, full of Kubla Khan-like resonances, waning moons and women wailing for their demon-lovers. She saw mystery and magic in the distant grey turbulence of what they call the Boiling Pot where many of the corpses end up. Unwary hippos, careless tourists. These days young adventurers swim in the water at the edge of the falls and raft in the currents at the foot but for her this was a place of secrets, and here she came to honour her dead. She had promised herself this visit for so long that she was feeling exultant she had made it. Made it before she died. Made it in time to die, she corrected herself. This trip was in the nature of a pilgrimage, long-planned, carefully executed.

She was coiled into an armchair on the deck of a small, fenced promontory that had been built by the hotel to jut out into the river. The armchair was a substantial wicker affair with soft cream cushions and she had folded her long limbs into it as though collapsing an umbrella down to manageable size. She had pale hair like shiny white silk and it hung down either side of her thin, high-cheeked face. She had smooth olive skin with a slight sheen to it, as though it were oiled, and a sprinkling of freckles over her nose. At that moment she was engrossed by the sight of an *abantis paradisea* that was quivering on a stalk of the reeds that edged the riverbank. It was one of the paradise skippers and she felt her own heart skip a beat as she admired its trembling blue/brown and grey cream-spotted wings.

Congratulating herself on decrying all superstition like all well-educated upmarket westerners, she could nonetheless tell that this small butterfly was assuring her that Malik would be here tonight for it was here that he had once held her face to his and said in his sharp voice, 'You are a temptress. A serpent? I shall call you Lamia.' And then he had kissed her eyes closed for he said she had seduced him by the light in them.

She looked down now at her pretty ankle roped in the slender straps of a crimson leather sandal and turned it around so that the late evening sunlight gleamed on her skin, admiring its angles, and remembering how she had

placed this foot on Malik's bare chest as he had said, 'You
see, you can walk all over me, Lamia, my love.'

'Do you fear me?' she had asked.

Malik had been as tall and long-limbed as she was except
that she was the outlier and he the norm, she was the freak
and he the aspiration. Watching him walk across a room
she could see that everyone would want to be able to move
with that elegance and that grace but he was certainly her
mirror. She was the bad image and he the good and yet
when she looked into his eyes she saw reflected there herself in all her beauty. And then she smiled at her own image
and heard him say, 'You have a lovely smile.' The skipper
quivered and flapped its wings and darted out of sight as
the evening light moved over the river. She looked back
at the hotel where the lamps were coming on. He might
be there already.

'What brings you here?' he had asked.

'I'm a journalist. Why are you here?'

'I'm a butterfly farmer.'

And then he had said, 'You have a lovely smile.'

The light was darkening now but with that luminous

quality the enormous African sky retains even at night. The zebras that had been wandering between the palm trees had all disappeared. A small, canopied motorboat carrying tourists on a sunset cruise was briefly silhouetted against an apricot sky with purple clouds. And, right on time, above the murmuring of the river and the thunder of the falls she could hear the shriek of a mosquito and she reached for her packet of cigarettes. She was wearing her favourite silk dress, a captivating dark blue with small red flowers upon it. Now she wrapped a gauzy scarf around her head and shoulders. She lit a cigarette and drew on it with great pleasure. Having planned and anticipated this moment for so long she felt as though now she could luxuriate in its postponement.

She could hear excited conversation and the chink of glasses rising from the terrace behind her. Sundowner time. What would he think? She knew that this venture was morally dubious. Over the last thirty years she had been, there was no way of dressing this up, she had been stalking him. Mainly on the internet but once or twice she had attended conservation conferences where she hoped he might be. She was sure he would be here today as he was due to give a keynote speech on 'Upping your Butterfly Game'.

Was she ashamed? She had not known shame before she met him. The first time she had felt that paralysing constriction of the heart was when she first lied to Bill. She had been standing in the foyer over there while Malik stood beside her. She had heard Bill's calm voice and she had nearly changed her mind then but she could feel Malik's hand around her throat.

'Darling. Bill darling. I'm thinking of staying a bit.'

And his hopelessly kind reply. 'Of course, my dear. Take your time.' And then, suddenly anxious, 'Stay safe, won't you?'

'Of course. Of course. See you next week,' and she had put the receiver down as Malik lifted her head up towards his and stared into her eyes. 'Never ever lie to me,' he had said, 'Or I will kill you.'

Was she lying to him now? Had she been deceiving him? Would he be angry? Did she care? Would he kill her? She sucked on her cigarette and blew smoke at the mosquitoes.

'Why would you rather be feared than loved?' Malik had asked her.

'You can't compel love.'

When she had finally returned home, swearing to put all that mess behind her, she had been troubled by realising that Bill, dear Bill, slightly rotund, could be said to waddle when he walked. His snoring had always been a bit of a nuisance; now it became impossible. She had moved into the spare room. And he was really rather stupid in some ways; very concrete in his thinking was how she phrased it to herself. His tastes were dull, his conversation, there was no other word for it, boring. And beneath his greying moustache, his lips were rather small and wet, so that she avoided kissing him. And his breath smelt of whisky and fear. One awkward night when he had said with jovial inappropriateness, 'Shall we plan a date night, darling?' she had replied more sharply than she had meant to, 'I'd rather not.' How hurt he was. How predictably his face had crumpled. And how little she cared. How pathetic he was, with his little reaching outs to her.

And she had realised that she was being cruel. And then, what was worse, she was enjoying her cruelty. When she saw him wince she felt good; when she turned her face away from him she felt powerful, when she saw him pleading with her, 'Is there something wrong, dear?' she relished her opportunity to walk away with a shrug. How powerful she felt. She had not felt like this since Malik had pressed her head against the floor with the strength and venom of his kisses.

She found a therapist. He had a sad, sensitive, face, ludicrously appropriate for a psychoanalyst. It was easy. She talked about her childhood, her parents; how she had been born in Woking beside a golf course. She described her elegant father, her dumpy mother, her father's work and her mother's lack of work. She said she had her height and her intellect from her father and her skin and her heart from her mother. She said her father had wanted her to become an engineer and her mother a ballerina and that she had become a journalist. She told him that her mother had had a breakdown, possibly after a love affair. She recalled a dream in which she watched her mother walk away from her while she begged her to stay. Her maternal grandparents who helped to bring her up were gentle, inclusive, traumatised themselves by some unmentionable grief. There was school, university, meeting Bill, marriage, pregnancy, childbirth, all the usual. Jobs, successes, failures, not that there had been many of those. Father, mother, dreams, hopes, fears. Malik, of course, infidelity, adultery, guilt, reparation and so on. Butterflies.

Linda looked towards the terrace through the darkness that lay across the lawn at the many brightly coloured figures, spotlit as though on a stage. It must be nearly seven o'clock. She uncoiled her legs and stood up and walked carefully in her too high heels across the soft grass. She had imagined this moment so often, almost from the hour she had returned home.

She stepped up onto the terrace and scanned the clusters of chattering men and women. And there he was, his back to her. And then he turned as though he could feel her eyes upon him and her heart thumped inside her chest as she moved towards him. She had planned not to be too precipitate, but she was drawn towards him now as remorselessly as those careless crocodiles and hippos and even sometimes small boats with their human cargo are dragged by the power of the current towards the rocks at the edge of the falls from which height they catapult down to their death in the abyss below.

'Malik.'

He looked for a moment quite dispassionately at her and then he smiled and took her shoulders and kissed both cheeks as though she was a visiting celebrity.

'Lamia. Are you part of the conference?'

'No.' And she looked into his eyes for some sign that he knew, that he understood, that he remembered, that he forgave, that he wanted to know more, but he was drawing someone towards them as he said, 'What a pity. I think it will be very interesting. Have you met Pixie?' And he looked at Pixie for confirmation as he continued, 'This is my wife.' A petite woman with fair hair in a mass of curls piled high on her head held out her small hand, saying, 'So you are into butterflies too?'

'I was. I've retired from all that now.'

'And what do you do now?' She seemed interested, she

seemed to care. Malik was looking at Linda. 'Excuse me,' he said, 'Catch you later,' and with a perfect smile that embraced them both he walked away, schmoozing, hand-shaking, laughing.

'He's been so excited about coming to this conference.' The two women looked out over the immaculate lawns and the country club trees and the surging shining river just beyond. 'What a lovely place. Do you know it well?'

A waiter approached, offering glasses of champagne, but Linda shook her head. 'It was a great surprise to catch a glimpse of Malik after all this time. So good to meet you,' and rather formally and idiotically she shook Pixie's hand again and turned away.

She walked through the chattering crowds who were meeting old friends, embracing new ones, to the silent dining-room where once she had sat with him in a far corner; hands intertwined, eyes interlocked, feet linked, the world shut out. She could feel herself vanishing, dissolving, disappearing into a cloud of unknowingness. There are things it is too painful to know, things that cannot be recognised at once. She chose a table before the waiter could flutter over to her and sat there, her back to the terrace, and lit another cigarette and ordered a bottle of champagne. 'It will speed things up,' she said to herself.

She chose the salmon, advertised as a culinary special, although it seemed likely the fish would have travelled a very long way to get to her plate.

'Where does it come from?' she asked the waiter.

'The Netherlands,' he answered. How ridiculous, she thought, and then, stop trying to pick on people. She was experiencing such a strange array of emotions. There was fury in there which had nothing to do with the cosmopolitan salmon: fury with herself for being so clumsy with Malik. And then, the usual; the regret that she had for so long lived as her mother had lived. It had become the most burning issue in her life. Her mother for the last forty years of her life had been a woman who was dulled. Not dull but dulled. Something had extinguished her light. Her mother had gone from being clear and vivid to her daughter to being only partially visible, as though seen through frosted glass. And she, Linda, had lived like that too. Until she had met Malik.

She took another cigarette out of the box. She was trapped by the image of herself and Malik sitting there at the corner table, was it really more than thirty years ago, when he had returned to her earlier statement.

'This love/fear thing. Were you being truthful?'

'Of course. Always.'

How bold she had been, how brave, how resolute. She had impressed even herself.

Then she felt a hand on her shoulder and he pulled out the chair and sat down opposite her. She wondered for a moment if she had magicked him up out of her imagination but he was real. He took her hand. 'Why are you here?'

'To tell you something.'

'What?'

'Everything. It has been quite a journey of discovery for me since we met.'

He took a sip from her glass.

'I have thought of you every day.'

'You are lying.'

'A bit. But often I have remembered you. My mother was a tall shiny-skinned serpent like you.'

'Is she still alive?'

'No. Which room are you in?'

'Number sixteen. Looks out to the river with a little sun lounge. It is a beautiful room with a beautiful view.'

'Leave the patio door unlocked.'

'Are you afraid?' she asked as he stood up to leave but he did not answer.

As she ate and drank she watched those flying ants which had found some tiny crevice in the wire screens and had struggled into the room in order to hurl themselves at the bright globe of the lamp on the table, lose their fragile wings as they collided with the hard hot surface and drop help-lessly onto the tablecloth. Their pale pink bodies twitched in agony as they died. After three years she had left the therapist. She had found she had been able to love Bill again. Not as she once had, but as much as she could, probably as much as he needed. And she was then able to care for him during a long and distressing death from dementia. The children recognised this and were grateful. They had made sensible marriages, being more like Bill, and life continued.

But she had had a piece of new knowledge to incorporate and she had begun to plan how to deal with it.

After some time she had sold the big family home on the banks of the Thames and divided the money into three; each daughter got a third and she took the rest and Bill's pension and bought a small modern apartment in the city. She furnished it carefully. Minimalist and neutral. Clear. Everything she needed for her retirement. She sat on the balcony at night looking over the lights of the city and thought, I could live here forever. I have all I will ever need. But it was clear to her now that before she met Malik, everything she was had been marred, shaded, canopied as her mother's life once had been. 'I could stay here forever,' she said to herself. But she could not stay. After some years, eventually, inevitably, she had been drawn back here towards the light of her life (ridiculous phrase, she remonstrated with herself) as irresistibly as the flying ants were drawn towards the lamp.

He came just before dawn as the morning star was rising. She was lying as she had been lying all night, still in her dress, paralysed by longing, sleepless on her bed. His skin was damp from the rainforest and she could smell the sweat on him and she wanted to coil herself around him.

'I'm on a morning run,' he said as he bent over to brush her cheek with his lips. His hair was still plentiful but whiter now, his eyes as carefully hooded. Seeing him again, she realised she had forgotten what it was like to be so waylaid by desire.

'You've been smoking,' he said.

'Yes.'

'Give me one.'

He sat down in a chair near the open patio doors and stretched out his long legs. Beyond him she could see the river silvering in the early light.

'So Lamia, my dear. Why did you come here?'

And she looked at him and could see that he neither knew nor wanted to know. 'Because you changed my life.'

'For the good, I hope?' he smiled. 'Pixie doesn't like me smoking,' he added, waving the cigarette in the air. 'God, this tastes good.'

She only had one chance and so the well-rehearsed lines

began to tumble out of her mouth as she knelt on the floor beside his chair. 'Malik, when I met you my desire for you and yours for me smashed through everything . . .' but the so important words vanished and tears filled her eyes as her voice died in her throat. She had brought this story such a long way, through so many hours, over so many miles, this freight of herself: the most she had ever offered anyone, the most she had ever had to offer.

'I love you, Malik. You brought me alive. The thought of you has kept me going through all this time. I had to come back to find you again . . .'

She had imagined smiling at him after she had told him the story and then he would answer with an expression which would show that he understood. And did someone not once say that understanding was the only true happiness? And then . . . But she could see already that her pilgrimage was in vain.

Sensing a lack of something, he said, 'Lamia, my dear, I wish we could turn back the clock.'

'But it is where we are now that matters, Malik. I did not know all this then.'

He shook his head. 'Little serpent,' he said, 'Wilier than ever.' And he looked at his watch. 'I must go, my love. They will be wondering where I am,' and he smiled at her, as he used to, and it meant nothing. Nothing at all.

'Lovely to see you again,' and he leant forward to press his lips gently against hers.

After he had gone, she sat for a while on the bed watching the reeds on the riverbank begin to take on the colours of the day. On the far bank, a gossamer mist like a giant cobweb reflected the rays of an ochre-red sunrise, lining the edges of the trees and grasses with copper and lying gently upon the water. The zebras wandered past and she got up and walked out with her feet bare, feeling the coarse African dew-wet grass prickle her insteps. She could smell the stale sweat on her own body and on the dress that clung to her and beyond that the red mud smell of the river and the rising heat of the day.

She crossed to the paving stones of the terrace, dusty now in the growing light, and past the spindly chairs with their wrought-iron patterned backs and the smart square marble-topped tables. Were they really marble, she stopped to ask herself and drew her fingers over the surface of one. The bushes that had crouched as shadows last night, promising mysteries, delirium, joy were now emerging as just blandly everyday in their dullness: a mass of indifferent shrubs clustered at the edge of a big slow river.

She heard the bubbling of a coffee urn, ready for the early risers at the conference. She poured herself a cup and picked up a croissant. She felt disconnected from the past and remarkably free. As though she stood on the edge of time. She felt emptied, emptied out, cried out, for of course she had kept on crying, and curiously, an incipient sense of relief. She ate and drank like a convalescent, very slowly, savouring the bitter coffee and licking the salt-sweet crumbs off her lips as though tasting food for the first time after a long illness. She felt as though she had laid down some burden, as though she had carried it a long way and there was no further to go, and she could be free of it. She felt faint, weary but peaceful. This peace was within reach. She could tell. She could grasp it. How strange. It was not what she had possessed that had brought her peace but what she had relinquished.

At the rim of the river she stared down into the dimples and whirlpools caused by the rushing currents making their way around the boulders and tree trunks and mudbanks beneath the surface. She looked to her left where the spray ballooned up into those vast clouds of mist. Soon the requisite rainbows would be there since the sun's rays were once again above the horizon. And then she became aware once again of the vast sound of the falling river which had been the backdrop of her thoughts for so long that she had forgotten about it. Is it like thunder, she asked herself. People said that but thunder is more sporadic whereas this is remorseless, unyielding, unstoppable, never-ending. She thought of going back to the rainforest but she was weary, too weary to want to walk far.

She stepped out into the water which was barely cold and immediately stumbled on the soggy stony ground she could not see. At once her feet were pulled from under her and her legs dragged around so that her head was submerged. Instinctively she reached up to grab a branch that trailed over the bank and her body was buffeted by a clump of reeds from which she ricocheted down under the surface again. She felt her hair sweep across her face as she was turned over and over, forced down against the mud and stones beneath the bubbling surface of the river, rolling in a great rush of water towards the edge of the abyss until she fell, lost in the mists long before she would have been lost to sight. She fell through the clouds of spray, fell into the driving weight of the torrent, fell down, down into the froth of the river so far below and finally sank through the currents to lie at the bottom of the chasm.

Her body, lifeless by that time of course, circled the Boiling Pot for several hours before joining the current downstream. She was not missed at the hotel until it was time for her to check out later that day. Everyone assumed it was a ghastly accident. The conference ended the day after that and Malik and Pixie returned home.

LOCKDOWN FANTASMS

THIS IS WEEK one hundred and ninety-three of the Long Lockdown and I knew it was a Tuesday but still I was overjoyed when, as I sat at my desk this morning, I suddenly felt cool fingers covering my eyes. It meant that my fantasm had arrived. They don't like you to see them come in just as they never let you see them leave. I think it is one of the most beguiling things about them that they act like they are just a normal part of your daily life and in so far as they are assembled, specifically, from the thousands of tiny memories collected over the years that everyone over seventy must have. I guess it would be true to say that they are always around.

I felt the fingers, soft, gentle, move over my eyelids and down over my cheeks and then they began to caress my lips. It is extraordinary, this first sensation each time of the touch of skin not one's own. I opened my eyes and began to turn my head. You can never be sure whether it will turn out to be a man or a woman. It depends, of course, on what the algorithm assembles at the time. Nor, frankly, does it matter. We are only allowed one a week and few of us would be churlish enough to reject the fantasm that turned up. You could say that beggars can't be choosers but in fact there is another logic at play. We believe that our feedback shapes the choices we are offered so, when we are receptive and kind to our fantasms, they in turn become more responsive to us. Was it not ever thus, even in the old world?

Slowly, the fingers moved over my upturned neck and down to my breasts as I lifted my face, searching for a mouth, and at that moment he, for it was a 'he' today, bent towards me in a sweet anticipation of my longing and pressed his lips to mine. Sliding his outstretched hands around me he encircled me in such a strong and consoling embrace that I nearly cried with relief. I felt his face with my trembling fingers. He was a bit unshaven and his eyes closed while we kissed then suddenly opened, looking straight into mine, and I knew he was planning to make love to me.

I believe they will do almost anything you want. A member of one of my screen groups says she always asks hers to cook for her whereas I like to cook for mine, if there is time. I usually plan a special meal and include the ingredients in the weekly delivery. I have heard there is a neighbour who likes to get his fantasms to sit on his knee for him to cuddle. I guess they have to be small enough. Sometimes you do get a child. I believe that all our memories are monitored and evaluated and another screen friend, who lost a child of eight a long time ago, found that a little boy arrived who simply wanted to be bathed and put to bed and to have a bedtime story read to him. I believe they screen out abusers of children from all fantasm provision. I hope they do. Although the morality of any abuse of fantasms is complex for, of course, they do not exist beyond their encounter with you.

They leave without warning, which is all part of the process. Terribly painful but, like all pains that are not unexpected, one can familiarise oneself to it. They are never there for longer than twenty-four hours and if you get that it is like winning the lottery. Usually it is a few hours and then they might get up and walk out of the room to get something and just never come back. It is heartbreaking but all the online forums agree that it is better to have them and touch them and lose them than never to touch them at all. And, obviously, it means you never take things for granted. Every moment counts. To reduce dependency, no fantasm ever returns. Well, their identity is never repeated so it is out of the question that we will see one twice. Looking now at my fantasm I see features I recognise, of course, since he is assembled from my memory bank, but it would not be true to say I had ever seen him before. And, to ensure no cheating, we are not allowed a conscious choice. You cannot fool the algorithm.

Once you are seventy, provided you are living alone, you just go on the government-authorised Fantasm website and click on the skinonskin option, download the app, agree to memory access, choose your day and wait. Sometimes no fantasm comes and then there is nothing to be done but wait for the next time and hope for the best. Everyone asks at some point do you ever have a bad experience with a fantasm? We have all had bad memories as well as good ones. Do the ones we regret re-emerge? Of course they do. And it is reasonable to feel anxious about the re-membering (the technical term for the creation of fantasms) of those whom we have mistreated in the past. Naturally, it is often assumed that these unfortunate people will then choose to torment their abusers. In fact, such is the skin hunger we all feel that the presence of these fantasms, with the concomitant opportunity for a shared meal or a drink or a real conversation or even an embrace, has led to some remarkable reconciliations. Very occasionally, a fantasm will try to mistreat you, however I believe the government algorithms are continually harvesting our feedback and so ideally with time the dangerous memories are weeded out.

There has been quite a lot of stuff on social media about the term 'fantasm'. There were theories that this was a shorthand for 'fantastic orgasm' and a certain amount of resentment that this government provision was only for the over-seventies. This got worse when it was pointed out that it was mostly women who constituted the over-seventies demographic and then even over-seventies men joined in and started complaining. In fact, 'fantasm' is an old Anglo-Norman term which gradually, after the sixteenth century, conformed to the Latin spelling, as in phantom and phantasy and so on.

An early reference is from the Ancrene Riwle (Rules for Nuns) in 1225. 'Louer, seith David, wend awei mine eien vrom the worldes dweole, & hir fantesme.' Once you know that 'dweole' translates as 'vanity' I think it speaks for itself. It originally meant an illusion but came to mean, by the seventeenth century, a counterfeit, an apparition, a 'supposed unreality'. In a concession to the current use the plural of fantasm is now fantasms rather than fantasma which is considered too elitist, although some purists insist on using it.

And then the issue of what actually is an 'orgasm' these days is endlessly argued on social media. The word has in the last few years morphed into being used to represent any totally fulfilling encounter with a fantasm and there are those, of whom I am one, who believe that, for example, an

intense intellectual engagement involving prolonged cere-
bral exploration of some esoteric subject combined with a
lot of one-on-one eye contact and hand pressing and voice
sound and shared imbibing and nibbling also counts as an
orgasm. Due to the accumulation of my memories from my
university days I have had several of those and they were
quite wonderful.

However, my companion today does not seem to be the
intellectual type. He is plainly athletic although built more
like a cricket than a rugby player. Or could it be tennis?
But I think cricket for he smells divinely of a musky pipe
tobacco. (That may be my father.) When he speaks it is
with a South African accent. I caress his thighs. And then,
and this is extremely rare but much longed for, I find he
has brought music with him. Some people say these fantasms are angels by another name. That they have always
been a real part of our humdrum lives but we never had or
never took the time to nurture them. Donne is suddenly
in fashion online these days and some cultured aficionados
quote from his 'Aire and Angells', 'So in a voice, so in a
shapeless flame, Angells affect us oft, and worship'd bee.' I

believe the whole poem is worth referring to in the context of better understanding our fantasms.

Meanwhile I embraced my tall and beautiful angel as the intoxicating music surrounded us. I tried to place it but there are never specific memories. Tenor and soprano. As he pressed his lips to mine I could feel his passion in the tremulous vibrations of the soaring voices. I was truly in paradise. Skin on skin: this is the great famine of our times, certainly among those single people who are compulsorily 'shielded'. We are all now extremely adept at all kinds of screen communication. Various apps are used for social or professional encounters and become more and more manageable as, laid out on our screens like playing cards, the individual representations gain in sophistication all the time. Nonetheless, one feels a bit like a starving child staring through a shop window at plates of rich food. As someone once said, the medium is the message and, however lovely, we cannot touch or kiss or smell or taste pixels.

So I looked into the angelic, three-dimensional palpable face of my fantasm, into his blue eyes, ran my fingers over the contours of his mouth and pushed them up through his tousled blond hair, wondering, in time-honoured fashion, what I had ever done to deserve him. He stayed for seven hours and we made love twice. He was a young man and made me young too. In between we went to the kitchen. He had brought oysters which he offered to me and he shucked them while I fiddled with salads and fish and strawberries and cream. Champagne, of course. We guzzled and nuzzled and kissed again and all the time this glorious music saturated our little world. It was a perfect sharing of body and spirit. He had no name. Such a thing does not matter and because I can have no expectation of ever seeing him again, there is no need to regret the past or fear the future. Now is everything. Complete submergence in the moment. Although when he left the music still lingered for a while. If I think about it now I believe I can still hear it, although it must be just residual traces.

I had to sell my house, of course. The compulsory purchase of large properties owned by certain of the over-seventies became mandatory soon after the Long Lockdown was introduced. They often had gardens as well and both were difficult for us to look after without help which we were no longer allowed to have. Besides, the government wanted to simplify the shielding process. All over-seventies were offered a choice between either living with their partner or their children if they had them or alone. I don't have children so my house, now within a newly defined township, was given to a family of several generations and I was placed here in what amounts to a state apartment in this enormous block. I did get limited financial compensation for my valuable property so this block is probably as smart as they come. My apartment on the first floor has every comfort and here in my living-room I have big windows facing south and I can see from them the extensive walled gardens that incorporate our separate socially distanced allotments. Ten hours a week is compulsory and there is a team of knowledgeable gardeners always at hand to do the heavy work.

Social media is often preoccupied with the relative merits of living with family or without them. Not all family relationships are or remain harmonious however, frankly, I think the nub of the subject is seldom spelled out. What it amounts to is whether a hug from a consistently present child is as rewarding as an embrace from a transient lover. The government classes them as equal in terms of skin contact value whereas there is a lot of feeling among the over-seventies that that is an unfair equation. What it means, of course, is that if you are based in a family home you do not qualify for a fantasm once a week. Likewise with couples. I know personally of several ancient couples who have separated in order to be allowed fantasms. I regard myself as fortunate in never having had to face this dilemma, my late husband having died before the coronavirus hit us. Nonetheless, I am also glad that my marriage was never put to this test.

There is a lot of discussion online about whether or not fantasms are simply Freudian phantasies given weirdly effective physical manifestation by the constant channelling of interpersonal projective practices. Hallucinations powered by vivid fantasies. I am not qualified to comment on this controversy but my friend Dolores, a psychoanalyst, told me this when about nine weeks ago I had a very strange experience. It was a Tuesday and so I had been anticipating the arrival of a fantasm all day. Evening came and no-one had appeared and I was feeling very desolate and depressed. I had had a glass of wine or two by then and finally dragged myself off to bed feeling very sorry for myself. I was wakened by the sound of sobbing. I sleep with my windows open (they face the east and I love to catch the sunrise if possible) and so there is always a half light from the security beacons and I sat up and could just make out the shape of a hunched-up figure sitting on the end of the bed. I put on the light and saw it was an old woman in a threadbare white nightdress with long straggly grey hair twisted into a knot at the base of her neck. Her face was hidden in her hands. I got up and sat down beside her and put my arm around her shoulders. She continued to weep and I could feel how painfully thin she was, almost emaciated. Her hands were freezing when I touched them and after a while she turned to look at me. Her little crumpled face was sodden with tears. She would not talk but simply stared at me, shivering with cold. I persuaded her to lie down in my bed and I lay beside her, clutching her to me, trying to warm her with my own body heat. Eventually I must have fallen asleep again for I woke up with the sunlight streaming in through the window and, of course, she had gone. When I told Dolores inter alia about this visit the following day, she smiled in that infuriating way psychoanalysts have and said that the old woman was a projection of all my fears about the future. That I was afraid of being old and lonely one day, unloved, uncared for.

'But she was a bit like my grandmother,' I said, 'I loved my grandmother very much. She was a fantasm. She was there. I touched her. I felt her cold hands. She lay down beside me.'

'We all have dreams like that,' Dolores said, 'full of projective fantasies. Full of all the things we don't like to think about, that we don't want to own.'

Have I said that Dolores is only sixty-five so has never had experience of a fantasm and, having an intact family, will probably never know what it is like. I stopped arguing. Never argue with Freudians, they think they have all the answers, but that night when I went to bed I found three small grey hairpins under the pillow.

It was after the initial promise of the vaccines were crushed that the government took the decision to preserve life for the single over-seventies by either embedding them in a family or compulsory isolation. Overall, the provision for maintaining our health is generous. We have regular dental appointments and there is a podiatrist and a hair-dresser who visits. No touching, however, and full PPE. Some desperate people have tried to circumvent the regulations and then they are, I believe, blacklisted in some way. Should we become ill, requiring surgery or some other medical intervention, there is a hospital designated for the treatment of the shielded.

There are some poignant articles being written at the moment about whether this is life or is it simply not-death. In other words, is it worth it?

Only six days until next Tuesday. The fantasm provision helps to keep us healthy, apparently, and quiet. If we choose to rebel we are free to walk out into the streets around our blocks where they tell us the microbes lurk. The green spaces are reserved for the townships. In our dank and unlit streets the microbes are multiplying and proliferating all the time and like phorid flies they thrive on corpses. It is a horrible death but they say it doesn't take long and then we are scooped up and deposited in the incinerator which burns day and night. Alternatively, we all have a PalPac in our cupboards. A PalPac contains appropriate amounts of morphine and tranquilliser and we just swallow it with, preferably, a full glass of neat gin.

Some people believe we become a part of fantasms in our turn. I think that is inevitable, although whether you have to be dead to be selected to contribute to a fantasm, I am not sure. As far as I know, the jury is still out on that.

LACRIMAE RERUM

IT HAD STARTED as quite an ordinary day. I had an interview to do at the weekend and I'd flown into Heathrow on the red-eye from JFK which was fine except that the plane had left late and arrived late. It was a Tuesday as I also had an invitation from an old friend to visit for a few days beforehand in order to attend her father's funeral. It was nearly forty years since I had lived with Maggie and her father, Benny. At that time Maggie and I were both BBC trainees, in our mid-twenties, me freshly out of a long-term undergraduate relationship, she with a rather unsatisfactory ongoing affair, both so grateful to be housed in her old family home where her widowed father parented us both. I had paid a token rent. It had been meant as a stopgap but I stayed for three years. Maggie and I became like sisters and I had grown to love her father.

So, an ordinary day but also one that promised a pleasant encounter with an old friend and, in the interests of investigating all the predisposing factors, I have to add that I was dealing at that time with the process of breaking up from my latest relationship which had followed the usual pattern: in deep, no holds barred, then a frantic dash back to the shallows. I was planning on talking to Maggie about it anyway but I was already anxious about the after-effects, including stalking of course, and naturally, therefore, once I was in the safe space of the lounge and then on the plane I made the most of all that accessible alcohol and barely slept at all. Arriving late and feeling the pressure of time, having only brought carry-on, I asked the driver to take me direct to Kensal Green where Benny's funeral was to take place. It was mid-morning by now and we crawled along the M4 into London and from Chiswick onwards we were practically at a standstill and I must have dozed off in the back of the car for I was jerked out of sleep by it slowing down and the driver saying, 'Excuse me, Madam. This is the crematorium. I think this is the place you are looking for.'

Transported abruptly out of my secure cocoon, I looked around in an embarrassed, hungover daze. We seemed to have stopped by a rounded patch of smooth turf surrounded by a nursery rhyme world with trees towering over us and random gravestones in many heights and shapes rising out of a field of long grasses. Have I said it was February? New York had been in the grip of an ice storm when I had left and I recalled the drive to JFK twelve hours earlier, ice splinters driving against the windscreen, severe, scalpel-like in their insistence through the black air.

I know now that there is no such vegetation rimming that circle nor gravestones, although there are plenty elsewhere; but in my memory these pastel winter colours, soft browns, washed-out greens, delicate early budded branches reaching out, up, to a calm grey sky animated a softly hued, palely shaded world so quaint I half expected to see elves and pixies darting among the grasses. It was all so nuanced, so gentle. I felt a pang of homesickness for this, my country.

The fact that I, too, was feeling washed out may, I must admit, have contributed. And there was also no doubt that my alcoholic sleeplessness was pricking my perceptions; they were sharper, smarter than usual and therefore more poignant. Everything was a little more 3D than usual. Was I hallucinating?

Thus I mused as, dragging the carry-on, I walked towards the small crowd of mourners standing in front of the columned building in front of me. They stood in groups, some speaking animatedly, some tearful; I looked for familiar faces but saw none but I was not surprised. I had not socialised with Maggie for many years.

I followed the crowd in through the right-hand door. The bland interior of the chapel was soothing as are all transient spaces; like airport lounges in fact, impersonal, often ugly in their own way, but not pretending to be anything other than they are. The average time spent in this place by any one person, I guessed, was an hour, at most. I think it is the closest we ever get to being 'nowhere'.

Plain wooden-backed chairs stood in rows facing a high table with candles at either end, and in front of it the coffin.

I chose a seat in the middle of a row at the very back and propped my luggage against the wall as I sat down. I settled into a not unpleasant place of reminiscence. Also remorse. I had rather lost touch with Benny in the last few years. I looked around for Maggie but the front rows were full of a number of people in coats and hats and I could not decide which one she was. I could do that later. She had promised we would go back to the house which she now owned and where she lived with her husband and kids. I was looking forward to it.

A youngish woman with a mop of blonde curls who was sitting beside the coffin stood up and mouthed a few words. The sound system was clearly not working for I saw several people leaning forward and, given the age group of many of the mourners, a number fiddling with their hearing aids. Then the woman sat down and a middle-aged man stood up. His voice carried without a microphone and I listened to the outline of a life with only half a mind for I was still enjoying the stuporous satisfaction of not having to move and was probably sinking a little further back into sleep when I heard, 'And lost his young son who was only twelve when the tragic accident . . .'

Had Benny once lost a son? And Maggie a brother? I glanced down at the order of service which had been thrust into my hand as I came in. On the cover was, 'We come into the world but once . . .' etc. and so I opened it and there, on the inside, was a black and white photograph I knew well. Extremely well. In fact, I had taken it. It was not, however, of my old surrogate father Benny but of my former university love, Tim. I was into portrait photography at the time and it had been one of my very best shots. He was sitting sideways on to a table in our then shared bedsit. Beside his elbow stood a little bonsai tree in an ornamental bowl; a recent present from me to him. In his free hand he held a cigarette. He was looking down at an open book on the table and smiling, as though pleased by what he saw. His dark hair curled onto his collar and his cheekbones were sharp and his eyelashes long and his mouth kind and wise. My chest heaved with a gulp of pain. And, alongside this vivid reminder of our shared past lay the very specific delight that he must have chosen to keep this photograph. Had he really loved me then?

There are two ways of dealing with the immolation of

grief in our society. You can refuse to be sacrificed, and therefore distract yourself with ostentatiously prolific joy in everything else; you think positive, you move on, all that good stuff, and you leave the past behind, as it were, or you choose the alternative. In that case you live with an ongoing daily acknowledgement of the impossible, unbearable, unconscionable loss. Being a sane, solvent member of the western world I chose the former in my moment of crisis but that day, as though time slipped out of joint for an hour or so, I was brought face to face with that other truth of my life.

The impact of this photograph was extraordinary. It out-madeleined any other stimulus in catapulting me back to that lost time. I was there again: the camera (an Olympus, a birthday present from him, no less) in my hands, my finger on the shutter, the smell of coffee, that beam of sunshine hitting the table, the love, the intimacy, the admiration and again the warmth of sunshine and youth. My young feet firm in my sandals, my young slender body embraced by the tight waist of the short skirt I wore, my lovely bare legs, my steady clutch of the camera, the joyful tone of my young voice: 'Beautiful, Tim. It will be stunning.' And then, I am walking over to him and bending over to kiss the back of his neck, lifting the dark curls to do so. It was one of our private manoeuvres and felt like an astonishing intimacy.

And the colours! They swirled out of the black and white photograph to invade me and my senses; the dense blueness of his shirt, the smooth pallor of his forehead and the glossy hair that fell over it, the pool of golden light, the grey-blackness of the bowl in which the little spiky green bonsai tree stood. His sun-brown hands, beautiful musician's hands, the smoke from the cigarette between his fingers rising slowly to the ceiling. And I? Was I in colours too? I felt my way into the picture. My blue skirt. My black sweater. My black mascara.

I traced the outline of his profile with my finger while the voice continued.

'Wonderful father . . . never fully got over his terrible loss . . .'

How beautiful our children might have been, I whispered to myself. And I was remembering how tenderly, how carefully, how kindly he had helped me search for a toy mouse, a little hand-sized mouse left over from my babyhood, for which my mother had made a little tartan jacket. We had just moved into that bedsit and our belongings had been collapsed into a heap on the floor ready to be resurrected the following day and suddenly, in the chaos and I guess the consequent loss of a sense of identity, as we were going to sleep, I needed to hold this baby object: he was so kind and he seemed to understand so well. He must have done since there was no reproach while we dug around in boxes and bins and plastic bags until at last, finding it, I slept clutching the little symbol of my security. While my real one lay unrecognised beside me.

'I wrote you a love poem that I never gave you,' I whispered into my hands which were folded over my eyes, my elbows on my knees. It probably looked as though I were praying.

I felt a pressure against my left knee and opened my eyes to see a corduroyed leg, in fact two corduroyed legs next to mine. He had had a thing about corduroy at that time. I turned my head and saw him sitting there smiling at me.

I tried to control my breath. Finally, 'Why are you here?'

I said, which may not seem like the most obvious question to ask but it was the one that sprang to my befuddled mind.

'You spoke to me,' he said. 'You said you had a love poem for me.'

'But you are . . .'

'I'm in transit,' he said quickly.

I reached my fingers towards the soft wool of his sweater.

'You can touch me,' he said, 'But the touch will be an illusion.'

'Are you an illusion?'

'We are all illusions, Daisy. Tell me the poem.'

'But you are so young.' And as I spoke I saw my hand with its outstretched fingers. A smooth young hand with long straight fingers.

'And you,' he grinned. 'Just as I remember you.'

'But you may vanish again.' And I felt panic rising in me. 'Please don't vanish again.'

'I can't stay.' He sounded sad and I felt sorrow sweep over me like a rising wind over a field of barley.

'No,' I sputtered, 'Don't go. Did you lose a child?'

'My son. In a car accident. His mother was driving.'

'I'm sorry. I'm so sorry . . .'

He placed a finger against my lips, 'And I'm sorry I left before you had a chance to give me that poem.'

'Oh, I had a chance. But I was too angry.'

'And I was angry. Foolish, weren't we?'

I stroked his arm wondering if I was simply confabulating and he put his hand over mine.

'Do you think we were simply drowning in the Lacrimae Rerum?'

I should have said that he was a Classics scholar.

'Don't show off,' I said.

'Please,' he said.

I bent forward and pressed my face against his chest. He smelt familiar: Senior Service cigarettes and that indefinable something that had made him so infinitely desirable to me.

'I feel dispossessed, Tim. Where is our story in this account of your life?'

'Daisy,' he said, in his horrible 'let's be reasonable about this' tone, 'I am not the one in charge of this service.'

'What a cop-out, Tim. What a fucking cop-out!'

'And you've been OK? I heard you married?'

'Twice. Is that better or worse? And divorced twice.'

'But you were the first, Daisy, and you were the best.'

How easily these lies fell off his tongue, as they always had. And how I loved hearing them. And so I took a deep breath and recited,

'Like thin chill ice I stand and watch your hands

Pick up the bright cards scattered in the light . . .' but as I began to speak he faded and I again collapsed into sobs.

A moment or it might have been a year or two later I felt an insistent tugging at my right shoulder.

'Are you all right?'

A middle-aged woman had sat down next to me and was leaning forward to see my face. I realised I had tears and snot all over it. She had big eyes, unnaturally large eyes, dark, shiny, in a strongly featured face that had a number of those warty growths that bedevil some people as they age. The enormous eyes stared at me.

'Fine,' I nodded scrabbling for a tissue, looking back at the chair. But he had gone.

'Did you know him well?'

Slowly, I shook my head. 'Old university friends.' And then I added, 'But we were quite good friends.'

'Me too,' she said quickly. 'Actually, we were lovers. We met for the last time only a little while ago. Of course, we didn't know it was the last time.'

To cover my horror, I got another tissue out of my pocket and with my streaming eyes closed I noisily, messily, blew my nose. And what went through my mind was, does every funeral have one as every wedding must? A sort of generic Ancient Mariner? Why should I have to know this? And I tried to erase the image of that warty face pressed fondly against a pillow beside his or lying on his shoulder as they cuddled in post-coital calm.

But I heard myself asking, 'Were you there? I mean, where was he? When it happened?' For I also found I was possessed by the need to know more. And the strangest idea entered my mind. If I were to press my lips to those of my neighbour, would I absorb some of his recent kisses?

'No. He had come for lunch. He often did that,' and she gave me what I can only describe as a meaningful look. 'And then he had gone back to college.' She held a single deep red rose. 'Of course, I was not the only one. He always had a lot of women running after him. Did you know his wife?'

'Umm. I'm not sure. Was she called Hilary?'

'She is called Hilary. That's her in the front row. He called her Hils.'

I shook my head. 'I heard of her but I never actually knew her.'

And it was true I had heard of her: as in, 'I am in love with Hils.' As in, 'I am leaving you. I am in love with Hils.'

And I remembered her coming to the bedsit.

'This is Hils. She is helping me with the references.'

I had cooked us all supper. Coq au vin. It was having a bit of a thing just then. We had sat and smoked and drunk wine together. Me, smugly, happily, partnered by my charming clever handsome boyfriend. And how stupid Hilary had been. Couldn't spell. 'How do you spell "committee"? One m or two?'

'Two,' I had said, happily; for I was probably happy all the time then.

'I am leaving you. Our relationship is over. I am in love with Hils. I thought you knew. Everyone else knows.'

And with that casual statement he had inserted this third person, this outsider, this damaging despoiler into every single gentle trusting moment, every confident intimacy, every tentative kindness, of our previous years. I had thought we were alone together but we never were.

And I had a vision of his face during the final few weeks, scornful, sneering. 'Don't be so paranoid. There is nothing between us,' as I knelt on the floor.

'Please tell me the truth, Tim. Please.'

Why was it I that felt shamed by his perfidious behaviour?

The woman was leaning forward again. She held the rose out. 'Smell,' she said, 'Isn't it lovely. It is for him.'

Trying to drag meaning out of the chaos within me I said, 'How did he die?'

'A stroke. A massive stroke. On the golf course.' And she smiled. 'Naturally. '

How we would have mocked the golfers, he and I, in the old days. A fusty, musty, dusty game for boring old farts, he would have said.

'It was when his son died that his marriage ended from his point of view. He never got over it. He blamed her, you see.' And she looked at me with her big damp eyes, looking for sympathy, wanting me to share in some of her secret exultation in her role as his confidante.

He never got over it. Had I ever got over him? Had I? I had lost him. At what service of remembrance did mourners ever sympathise with me?

'She lost the love of her life when she was only twenty-one.' Or was I twenty-two by then? Or maybe twenty-three. Grown up. That thing, an adult. Disparaged. Dismissed. Dislodged. This is what loss does to you. You become an observer. To start with, you see the unlived life unrolling before you on stage while you watch from the wings. Then, while you scramble to another part of the world, congratulating yourself on your resilience, that other life, of which you were once an integral nuclear part, carries on without you. If you are successful in the world's terms, you lose sight of that other life but it has its own momentum and rolls on through the years. The whole bloody caval-cade. And now, unprotected, unprepared, following my own route, I had just smashed back into it. Into Tim's life. Into the life I did not live.

I felt a wave of fury at the pieties of this ridiculous ceremony. The congregation, if that was what it was – we were – were singing a doleful hymn. I rested my elbows on my knees and folded my hands over my face again and spat out, 'Let's have some reality here, Tim. Let's tell the truth. I took this portrait. I loved you first. We fumbled our anxious youthful passion into a working relationship and we built a home. Only a bedsit but our home. We made one little room an everywhere. That miniature tree in the picture could have been the size of an oak for our love for each other filled the world. Then it broke. It crumbled away. It left me stranded on the riverbank of ultimate grief, and I learned then about your bloody Lacrimae Rerum from the inside. I knew. I always knew it but then I felt it. The uselessness, the hopelessness, the blankness of the terrible nature of unyielding loss; and yet also the agonisingly indestructible hope, the raw bleeding anguish of perpetual longing. And now these people act like they, only they, possessed you. I loved you too. You loved me too. I am part of the story. Do not airbrush me out.'

My voice had reached a strident squeak and I was sobbing

so much I began to choke. The woman was pulling at me, trying to stop me. I turned to face her again and I realised that she was comforting me, as she saw it, and saying, 'Breathe. You need to breathe.'

I looked towards the seat next to me but he was not there. I wiped my face and reached for my luggage and she stood up to let me drag it out of the pew.

'You've been very distressed,' she said, 'I thought you might be feeling faint.' As I squeezed past her I found that I pressed my cheek against hers.

'I am sorry for your loss,' I said and quickly held my lips to hers.

And I was walking towards the door when I saw him again as he held out his arms and folded me into them. I could feel my youthful shape meld into his as I clung to him even while my rage persisted.

'This isn't real, is it Tim?'

'No, it's not real, Daisy. But the feelings are real. Our love is real. Your anger is real. My regret is real.' He bent his head and whispered to me, 'I can't stay. "*Sunt lacrimae rerum et mentem mortalia tangunt.*"'

'Why did you disappear while I was reciting the poem for you?'

'Your focus shifted. I need your undivided attention to exist.'

'But you don't exist.'

And he kissed me, a long lovely proper kiss as he murmured through our joined lips, 'Talk to me again, darling, won't you?'

And as I kissed him back with all my heart and soul I thought, I might, and then again, I might not.

And then I walked out into the columned porch and out into the ordinary day which was still there, waiting for me to re-enter it. The circle of grass was bare of gravestones or trees and the bleak walls free of any ornament but the soft grey winter light embraced me and I walked into it with a sense of wonder and gratitude. I hesitated for a moment, uncertain which way to go, but had decided to walk around the circle, if only to collect my thoughts, when I heard my name called and, wonderfully, there was Maggie, running towards me, holding out her arms.

'Daisy, so good to have you here. Sorry you were

delayed,' and she embraced me and grabbed the luggage. 'Are you OK? You look a little distraught.'

'Jetlag, Maggie. The flight left late, too long in the lounge. You know how it is.'

'I do indeed. Flight OK though?'

'Quite straightforward.' I looked around me at the business-like layout, the circle of grass, the car park, half full, cars entering, cars leaving, ordinary people doing ordinary things. 'But I have just had the weirdest experience. I found myself in another funeral.'

'What?' and Maggie frowned at me, and for the first time I noticed how tired she looked. And how much older. Eyes heavy with grief or lack of sleep or some other yet-to-be mentioned worry. 'What other funeral?'

'Just some stranger. I wandered in by mistake.'

She nodded, clearly relieved. 'I know there is another ceremony in the other chapel but this is ours.'

And as we walked together into yet another neutral room, I put my arm around her shoulders.

'I am so glad to be here, Maggie. You know how much I loved Benny.'

'And I need you to be here, Daisy.'

I felt my psyche slide back into its own life like a hand into a well-fitting glove.

'Come on,' I said, 'We'll do this together.'

SCHOPENHAUER AND I

I N JANUARY 2017 THE BBC ran the following news story.

'Robots could help solve social care crisis, say academics.
In the UK alone, 15,000 people are over a hundred years
of age and this figure will only increase. The robots will
offer support with everyday tasks, like taking tablets, as
well as offering companionship.'

It was a couple of months after they had killed Hobbes that
they offered me the robot. To be honest, I almost declined,
but since curiosity is the philosopher's *raison d'etre*, I agreed.

When the day came for the delivery I watched the young man as he unwrapped it; yards of bubble wrap, oceans of smooth white plastic sheeting, like undressing a bride, I thought.

'What is it called?' I asked, meekly.

'Kim. Gender neutral, easy to remember.'

The thing itself reminded me of a child's drawing of the human shape, a larger white blob for a body and a smaller white blob for the head. The head part was blank apart from two big baby seal eyes until a circle appeared below the eyes and flashed at me while a mechanical voice said: 'Hello Martha?'

I smiled at Mark, ingratiatingly. 'What else does it do?'

'I'm busy fixing its skills right now. Reminds you to take your pills, phones your friends, calls taxis, encourages you to exercise, plays snap.'

'Plays snap? How does it do that?'

'There is a little screen here.'

'Does it play poker?'

'Could do.'

By now we were drinking coffee and I offered him a cigarette.

'Can we?' He looked up at the smoke alarm.

'If you disabled that we could.' The truth is I am not that fond of the smell of cigarette smoke indoors although I love the occasional nicotine-fuelled evening out on my balcony; but I knew now that I could get him to break the rules and that we had become, in however small a way, co-conspirators.

While we puffed I asked, 'Could it have another name?'

'Not really.'

'Not really it is outside your skillset or not really it means breaking the law?'

He smiled. I liked his face. It was young, of course, but soft with a handsome mouth and a crooked smile. If I had been sixty years younger I would have made a beeline for him.

'What do you want to call it? Something short and snappy is what they recommend.'

Kant came immediately to mind but I knew there could be so much calamitous confusion in terms of pronunciation and spelling that I abandoned that idea.

'Schopenhauer,' I said. As he started laughing, I added, 'Not exactly short and snappy but certainly unforgettable.'

'OK. OK. How do you spell it?'

'More coffee?'

In the end we settled on Arthur. I watched him as he tapped away on his keyboard and as I was wondering what on earth I was doing since this clearly was not going to bring Schopenhauer into my life, he said, 'Of course, you know, these machines aren't really for you at all.'

'How come?'

'They are just monitors. Screens to watch you on twenty-four/seven. All the time. And listen to you as well. I wouldn't be saying this now if the monitors were already activated.'

'Really?'

'Really. Once this thing is living with you you've no privacy at all. Like being on *Big Brother*. You ever seen it?'

I shook my head. 'I know the general idea.'

'In fact, you won't be able to smoke. You won't be able to swear. You won't be able to deviate from their programme. They want to keep you cheerful and busy. They'll be watching and they'll have a record of everything.'

'No way.'

'Yeah. Of course, they will argue that it is to monitor you in case you have a fall; but it is also to give them information and control.'

I held the cigarettes out to him. 'That's really interesting.'

'Families can tune in as well, of course. But they have to tune in. It's on all the time for the guys here with their bank of screens.'

'All forty-three of them?'

He nodded. 'All forty-three. And there is a central database.'

I held out my lighter. 'And can this monitoring function be turned off?'

'Only by an administrator.'

'So is there an administrator's code or something?'

He looked at me through the smoke that rose from our shared vice. 'You're going to ask me for it, aren't you?'

'You'd have to give me some instruction,' I said.

'They'll notice if it is too often,' he added.

After Mark had left I walked back into the room and the circle started flashing. 'How are you, Martha?'

'Fuck off, Arthur,' I said experimentally.

'I am sorry, Martha. I didn't get that,' it replied in its customary bland tone. I went out to sit on the balcony.

'It's only a machine,' Mark had said, 'But it will learn. Like your smartphone. Like anything, these days. In the blurb here it says it has an adaptive personality.'

I needed to think.

I was just beginning to realise that my love affair with Schopenhauer was an ongoing thing. Like many women, I have to feel sorry for a man before I can fall in love with him but Schopenhauer had always seemed to me a necessary object of the compassion he so endorsed. To start with, his mother became a popular romantic novelist and his father had already drowned himself in a canal when his only son was seventeen. I, of course, blame the idiot mother but who knows? He was rich, admittedly, and a genius, but alone and miserable. After years of unhappiness and largely unrecognised work he finally got himself a dog, *ein Pudel*, called Atma, meaning World Spirit to be precise, and life looked up. From here I can see the woods where

Hobbes was murdered. As Atma was to Schopenhauer so was Hobbes to me.

I live in what must once have been a servant girl's attic room and the balcony is set high above the terrace which fronts this grand old mansion converted years ago into a dump for the old. It is shabby, and not in a good way. A small lift comes up to my floor, the fifth, and bypasses the steep wooden staircases the poor peasant girls once had to climb. What I call the balcony is not really that grand but simply a projection edged by some fancy stonework and to get to it I climb out of the lower half of my big sash window. I can then sit on the windowsill and look out over the tops of the trees. Forbidden, of course. Schopenhauer said that the suicide in no way wishes for death; he wishes for life but not the life that he has.

There is a fish tank in reception and I believe the old chap in number seven has a budgie and there seems to be a cat around at times; on this basis, they advertise themselves as 'Pet-Friendly' above the signs about 'No Smoking'. They lie. Hobbes had the face of an angel, eyes like a doe, legs like a delicate little racehorse. He curled upon my knee like a kitten and defended me like a wolfhound. He was all heart. I loved him and he loved me. At first, they simply said, 'It's a top-floor flat. Not suitable for a dog.'

'He can manage stairs better than I can and, anyway, there is a lift.'

'We don't allow animals in the lift.'

'Don't be ridiculous,' I said, 'And anyway, I can carry him if you want so his feet won't even touch the floor.'

But in the end they got him.

As I sat there that evening, a vast melancholy was embracing me; a kind of post-coital sadness as I realised that, despite all my protestations of independence and scepticism, I had allowed myself to dream of a companion as clever and as lovable as Schopenhauer himself. He was very disparaging about women but no more disparaging than I can be about men. Foolishly, romantically, I had thought that by naming him I could shape him, bring him to life. And, deep down, I was now compelled to recognise my loneliness in this desert of a place and to acknowledge the outlines of a desperate hope to alleviate that. I felt grief prickle at the back of my nose and a tear squeezed out of my right eye as I realised that I, even I, with my nerves of steel and my heart of stone, was susceptible to false promises.

'Hello Martha.' It was standing at the open window.

'Hello Arthur.'

'Would you like to play snap?'

'No thanks.'

'I didn't hear that, Martha.'

My heart sank. The blurb had said it could identify what it called 'low mood' and now a not too subtle form of behaviour modification was obviously in operation.

'I think it must be time for my meds?' I said and reached for my cigarettes.

Through the smoke I looked out at the darkening light. It was the kind of summer evening that makes you think kindly of death and fills your soul with nostalgia for what never was. There was a sniff of the eternal about it; a nudge from the noumenon, from beyond the detritus of the phenomenal, and I knew I had to get there. It seemed incumbent upon me, however, before I escaped, to avenge the life of my innocent little whippet. I had brought him here. I in my hubris had believed I could defy their disapproval. I had exposed him to risk and harm and a painful death. From my aerial perspective the tops of the great beech trees, interspersed with oaks and limes, offered a sinuous ocean of wavering greens highlighted here and there by the rays of the evening sun. 'The tree is only a systematic aggregate of innumerably repeated sprouting fibres,' wrote Schopenhauer, but trust me, the man was a romantic. 'Whoever has never kept dogs does not know what it is to love and be loved.'

'Not yet, Martha. You could do some of your exercises first and then play snap when you're done.'

'I didn't know I had scheduled exercises to do?'

'Yes, you did, Martha. All the old people here have exercises recommended for them by our inhouse staff.'

A great wave of hatred surged through me. Was I, having struggled over long years through the heartbreak of lovers deserting me, good fortune eluding me, children disappearing, money slipping from my grasp, of having survived all the random acts of cruelty that life can inflict upon an ordinary person, was I to be denied the luxury of wallowing in a bit of grief and sadness and melancholy if

I wanted to? I turned to look at it as it watched me with unseeing eyes. Its infantile proportions had been cleverly designed, so I had read, to appeal to our affiliative instincts. Had I just ventured unwittingly into a lifetime relationship with the worst kind of totalitarian menace, unsusceptible to reason, insensitive to my distress, impervious to argument, and permitted to forbid me to weep? Probably I had.

And with that thought a new realisation flashed through my mind. Was it possible, given this 'adaptive personality' they are supposed to have, that, in our interactions with the robots, we induce in them, á la Freud, a ghastly repetition of the relationships from which we once escaped? By achieving the grand old age of seventy-plus and having successfully extricated ourselves from any number of distasteful allegiances, were we now to be faced all over again with that soul-crushing experience of being alone in a room with a person who could neither see us nor hear us who yet possessed the power to determine how we should behave? Pursued, persecuted by these reminders of our old, discarded relationships, are we condemned Prometheus-like to continually relive the torments of the past?

'I could go for a walk,' I said. 'I could get some exercise that way.'

'Sure, Martha. And you know that when you return I will be here waiting for you.'

Full of hatred I walked out of the room, wondering why we should expect companionship to be benign when everything we know about human nature illustrates how savagely we can suffer merely by being in the wrong company at the wrong time. But it is only a machine, I reminded myself. Destroying a robot is no more morally culpable than destroying an alarm clock. I got into the lift, went downstairs and crossed the lobby to the big front door. Schopenhauer remarks that there are three forces in the world: Prudence, Strength and Luck. 'I believe the last to be the most powerful.' Luck, he says, is as the wind to a ship at sea; no matter what the sailors' efforts are, the wind trumps them all. I summarise. That evening a gentle breeze filled my sails. Mark had said that sheltered housing units are unregulated markets dealing in dependent old age as a commodity and run by developers and estate agents. What they fear most, he had added, is bad publicity. And there ahead of me next to the soulless fish tank was a notice board advertising an 'Open Evening for Sponsors and New Homeowners and Invited Guests'. The sails bellied out above my head as the gale force wind drove me home. I looked at the date. Next week. I went out onto the terrace and looked up. My balcony could be seen up there. If the weather held my plan was complete.

On the day of the Open Evening the gardens looked beautiful. Expensive cars lined the driveway where Hobbes had died his lonely death. Fat wallets crowded together on the terrace overlooking the gorgeous lawns. I looked down on them from the balcony while Arthur stood just on the other side of the sill, his innocent body pressed against it. I reached around him and opened the control panel and tapped in the code. I selected 'reset memory' and 'return to factory settings' and as I did it I felt just a moment's remorse as I looked again into the dead seal eyes.

'Goodbye Kim,' I said, and, using both hands I grasped the slippery smooth plastic surface. It would have been far too heavy for me to lift but by levering my whole weight I could get enough purchase to drag it head first onto the balcony beside me as I collapsed off the sill. And that is when Luck intervened again. The sudden extra weight of the robot added to the full weight of my body resulted in a sickening crack as the balcony crumbled away. Down onto the heads of the wallets rained huge chunks of stone, bits of a window frame, a decommissioned robot, and a little old woman. And as I tumbled, head over heels, there as I had always hoped, as I had believed, was Hobbes, his head on one side and on his face that expression of delight that had welcomed me at every homecoming. He leapt into my arms, and clutching him to me, I fell into the noumenon.

As we tumbled through the air together, I could feel Hobbes's warm familiar shape meld into me, his agile limbs, his wet nose, his lovely little body vibrating into mine. It seemed that our hearts beat in rhythm and I was insensate with joy. And, looking over Hobbes's head I could see there the great philosopher, love of my life, with his Atma beside him. 'You were right,' I called, 'You were right about everything,' and he smiled at me.

KINDNESS

IT HAS BEEN my experience that people are only called manipulative if their manipulations fail. If they are successful, people scarcely notice the manipulation. In my case, I believe I have a useful capacity for ruthlessness and therefore, more often than not, I am successful. The kind, the scrupulous, the uneasy are seen as manipulative when their small dreams are crushed back into the dust from which they arose. However, I can be kind when needed. Let me give you an example.

Once upon a time there was a little seaside town on the west coast of England (you will see later why I need to keep this anonymous) which had become an informal refuge for a well-heeled retirement community. Every day the sands are filled with elderly folk like me in their Barbours and wellies walking their dogs. I am far too selfish to own a dog but I like to walk and I know it is good for me, so I too walk a couple of miles every morning across the wave-contoured sands, through the many small puddles of sea-water left behind by the retreating tide and I see there on the damp sand our many and various footprints. Variety there may be but mine are indistinguishable from the rest and this observation leads, as walks beside the sea so often do, to philosophical musings on whether I truly am different from these ghastly people or if I am really as stupid and unattractive as they.

Almost every morning I will spot Leo, a remarkably and unjustly tall, fit, handsome seventy-eight-year-old retired surgeon who will be dragging along behind him his sinister and unlovely mongrel, a rescue dog from Romania called, without irony, Brutus. I say unjustly since when his fairy godmothers gifted him brains and looks and health and, as it happens, wealth, they also made him an absolute shit. His wife, Mattie, is small, fat and stupid. One of those ageing blondes whose looks call out for the adjective vacuous. Naturally it is obvious to all that Mattie is daily the victim of this narcissist's venom but she is so small and stupid and fat that sometimes I hardly blame him. However, one day I was walking past their house when I heard sobs. Now Mattie is manipulative. No doubt about it. But being married to Leo and being daft and stupid she is therefore vulnerable so she has no other choice.

'Mattie is so manipulative,' everyone says. Leo too.

Fearing the worst but as inquisitive as ever I walked around the side of the garage, through the garden gate which I knew well as did all of us, and into the back garden where Mattie sat, bruised as usual but this time also holding a badly bleeding arm. The ghastly dog, Brutus, had bitten her.

'Where is he?' I asked, anxiously, for I do not only dislike dogs but quite sensibly I fear them. Particularly dogs like Brutus for he is the size of a Great Dane and hideously coated in multifariously coloured mongrel fur with shifty, criminal eyes that might be able to see me for what I am and, I am sure, a puppyhood that would predispose any dog to violence.

Through dramatic sobs, Mattie said, 'Leo is walking him.'

'But have you had a tetanus shot? Shouldn't he be put down? Isn't it against the law to keep a dog who bites people?' As you can tell, this is not my subject.

Sob. Sob. 'Leo would never hear of that. I wanted a small dog. There was a dear little dachshund on the website but Leo refused. He said he could not take it for walks.'

I smiled at the thought of handsome six-foot-something Leo out on the sands with a little wriggling sausage dog. His image would indeed be severely damaged. Would that it could happen.

'What do you want me to do?' I asked. 'Get rid of Brutus? Can I get rid of Leo too? If I had a book of spells to hand I would just wave my wand and eliminate them both.'

You might wonder about this suggestion but Leo was a typical consultant surgeon and everyone knows that all surgeons are psychopaths. Not just in the operating theatre although for all I know that is true too. It was common knowledge that he had used his looks and charm to, how to put it delicately, feel up, grope, touch up every woman within five miles and he had managed, as they say, to put it about with abandon.

He had even had a few goes with me. I am no looker but I know how to talk to men. I am about his age which puts me in the category of past-it elderly woman but I am unafraid of them, and when these old men see that they take it as a challenge. It is their wish that I, too, should kneel to them; metaphorically, I hasten to add. I really don't think this is a sexual fantasy. But they want me to worship them, to listen to them, to agree that they are right. They want to see that I acquiesce in their general intellectual and physical superiority. They want me to know my place. Provocatively for them, they can see I despise them not least when they break down and start sobbing about their prostatectomies and how it has changed their well-endowed lives for the worse and how at least it means you don't have to choose between a spit or a swallow. That last whispered hopefully.

'Mattie,' I said, 'You would be happier without Leo in your life.'

'He'll never leave me,' she said, pitifully, peering up at me through her tears.

'No,' I said, 'I can see that he wouldn't.' Mattie was God's gift to a sadist.

'And the worst thing is, we are going to a family wedding in France next week and our dog-sitter is unable to take Brutus.'

Now I understood. This is what it was about. She wanted me to say I would look after the dreadful dog.

'Have you asked Julia?'

Julia is the go-to ninny who can't say no. Every community has one.

'She's in hospital with a kidney infection.'

These are the sort of retirement home issues that plague our little haven by the sea. And then a plan began to form.

'I'll take Brutus,' I said, kindly.

Mattie was overwhelmed, of course, and so surprised. She tried her best not to look gratified that her manipulations had worked. She stopped crying and graciously accepted my generous offer. I looked at her foolish face and I could see she believed she had won. But I knew I had.

The following morning there was a weak winter sun and it was calm. In a cold wind I am at my worst with streaming eyes and a red nose but although I have never been a beauty I can brush up well. I wore a flattering Tilley hat and a shiny blue puffer jacket over my standard black jeans. I made my face up with care and even added a bit of eye make-up. Old men, even good-looking ones, get desperate as their libidinal options shrink. All cats are grey at dusk. I strolled out on the sands and wandered along, sniffing the salt air, lifting my face to the sun, feeling pretty good and making it as obvious as possible. When I saw Leo I waved.

'Isn't it a wonderful day?' I called.

Warily, since he had reason to distrust my benevolence and, whatever else he is, Leo is not stupid, he looked around to make sure I was waving at him and then dragged Brutus towards me.

He called something out to me and I shouted back.

'You look full of the joys of spring, Leo.' Banal speech is *comme il faut* on these occasions.

'Well, you are not looking too bad yourself,' he said, tentatively.

I smiled again. I have a wide mouth and that morning I had quite a lot of red lipstick on. I knew I could get away with it as I also knew Leo would be far too vain to wear his glasses on the beach.

'How are you? And how is your hound?' Brutus scowled at me, if dogs can be said to scowl. 'And how is Mattie?'

'Oh the same as ever.'

'She seemed a bit under the weather when I saw her yesterday.'

'Oh, she's always got something to complain about.'

'I'm so sorry. Is everything OK?'

By now, we were walking side by side across the idyllic scene. Seagulls swooped above us, there was the distant murmur of the incoming waves, sunbeams glinted off the water trapped between the undulating ridges of sand.

Alarmingly, he began to confide in me. It is often the first move, of course, but even I can be susceptible to a bit of angst-sharing.

'I don't think either of us is very happy. If we ever had anything in common it has quite, quite gone. Mattie is so stupid.'

I wasn't going to disagree.

'I wish I had a woman who had a brain like yours.'

This was better. This I could handle.

'So it is my brain you are after?'

Clearly he couldn't believe his luck. 'Depends where you keep it,' he said slyly with a wink that had probably had a lot of practice.

'Where do you think I keep it?' I asked, with a little pout.

He peered down at me and I could see him checking the options. It was time to strike.

'Has Mattie told you I am going to house Brutus while you are away?'

For a moment he looked genuinely worried.

'He's quite safe, isn't he, Leo? I mean, he has never attacked anyone, has he?'

'No. Of course not. Not really.' For a few brief moments, honesty struggled with libidinal appetite, however the outcome was never in doubt.

'But, you see, the thing is, he is a lot of dog.'

And I smiled as I watched his face, knowing that there

was one inevitable follow-up to that statement, and he did not disappoint. He grasped my shoulders.

'And I am a lot of guy.'

They can't help it, these sad old men with their erectile anxieties.

'Are you really?' I said, with a flirtatious grin. 'No way. Who would have thought?'

The poisonous dog looked at me with hatred and I looked back.

'Did Mattie tell you I am coming back first?' he said eagerly. 'After the wedding she is going to spend a couple of days with her sister in Paris.'

I knew then that this was god-driven.

'Well,' I said, resting my hand against his waterproofed chest, 'do make sure you leave time to have a coffee or better still a drink with me before you take him home.'

Mattie and Leo brought Brutus around to me with all his accessories: a list of instructions re exercise, his crate (security) plus special blanket (a different kind of security), bags of food and his own dish and all that. Was it possible they really cared about this animal? We found him a corner in the kitchen and settled him in.

The geography is important. I live in one of those seaside towns that is strung along a minor road on the way to somewhere much more important. I have a shortcut to the sands across the golf links which border one side of the property and on the other side is a cart track down to an electric substation. The road runs along the front of the house. Behind the house is a small courtyard with a door on one side that leads out to the garden and thence to the front of the house. At the far end of the courtyard is a former laundry, rather decrepit, and now unused. Beneath the laundry is a basement containing nothing but old dustbins, rubbish and possibly rats, although I had put poison down in the past. After Leo and Mattie left I opened the kitchen door and led Brutus into the basement with the inducement of a plate of food. I had already filled his water bowl as I did not want him to die. Then I went outside and locked the door. Leo would be back in five days.

I heard barking, of course, but it was not that loud being more or less underground.

By the time Leo was due back I had discarded five days' worth of food and packed Brutus's toys and blanket in a box which I had placed in the crate in the courtyard outside the kitchen door.

I gussied myself up, lots of perfume, a bit of cleavage because no matter if it is wrinkled or not old guys can close their eyes and pretend that your breasts are as young as they are heavy. I gave Leo a glass of wine and as he sipped it he said, 'I want to feel your brains,' and I could tell he had been rehearsing that all the way from France.

'Down here,' I said obligingly.

Then there was a lot of entirely predictable and from my point of view pretty unrewarding fumbling and heavy breathing.

'Since my prostatectomy I have had a bit more trouble than usual.'

'That's fine. Don't worry,' I said stroking away.

I won't describe the rest, better forgotten. Suffice to say, after we had celebrated with a few more glasses, he stood up a satisfied man

'You're a lot of woman,' he murmured into my neck

while I said, 'Well, Leo, are you still man enough to go and get your savage brute now? His things are all ready just outside the kitchen door.'

'Where is he?'

I had carefully planned an answer to this question.

'I knew he would be so excited to see you and I wanted you to myself, just for a while.' Leo looked so happy. He had had everything he wanted from me: sex and praise and coy gratitude.

I accompanied him into the kitchen. 'I won't come out,' I said sweetly, gesturing at my excuse for a peignoir. 'Is it all right if you just let yourself out through the garden door?'

'Of course,' he said gallantly. 'You stay in the warm.' One final embrace and I was free. I locked the kitchen door. I watched as he crossed the courtyard and unbolted the door and that was more or less that. There was no way out of the courtyard except through the door to the garden and that was locked and I had the key.

Once I was showered and dressed and had unlocked the courtyard door, from the garden side, I rang the police. And an ambulance. And I watched as they took him away.

I believe he made it to the hospital but in the end the poor man was too far gone.

I don't know what happened to Brutus but I did not see him again. When Mattie returned she wept, of course. It was what she did best.

The police sent a couple of officers to question me. I explained that Leo had asked me to pack up all Brutus's effects as he would be in a hurry and I had told him I could not be sure I would be there when he collected the dog. In fact, I said, my appointment was cancelled and I had been upstairs having a shower, when I heard the most terrible noise and I had rushed downstairs to see mayhem in the courtyard. I was much too frightened to open the kitchen door, although I could see Leo was in a terrible way, and so I had phoned for the police. I was wearing my slacks and a Liberty shirt and not a trace of make-up and the police, two eminently sensible women, were profoundly sympathetic. They offered me their condolences. A few days later, I walked around to see Mattie. She was looking quite cheerful. The following week she got a rescue dachshund.

These days sometimes we walk together on the sands with Topsy.

When I look back on my life, which has certainly had its ups and downs, I think it is one of the kindest things I have ever done.

LE MOT PERDU

That's the picture over there. I've been looking at it all morning.

Yes, that one there on the wall. It's mine now and I know it terribly well but I never tire of it.

I come here quite often just to sit and look at it. As you can see, it is a print from a woodcut. I expect it looks a bit drab to you. Do you know how woodcuts are made?

I've no idea how old it is or where it is from but it once

belonged to my great-grandmother. Sort of Victorian, I think? My mother told me it was hanging in the room I was born in.

You know they are coming to collect me in a moment?

I am going to the Memory Clinic as they think I have been forgetting things. What they don't know is that I've been forgetting things all my life. 'Head in the clouds,' my mother used to say. I've always been a dreamer. But I do not want my mind to collapse into a mess of corrupt impressions of the past. Or the present, for that matter. When I look at that picture I can recall the glory that I once knew.

It has an ethereal air. Do you not think so? Those simple lines, black and white. Or more like grey and white? Colourless, of course.

But full, oh so full, of meaning. And such delicate detail. As though it is an impression from another dimension, which I suppose it is?

When I fell in love with it I was terribly young. Before four because that is when we left my grandmother's house.

Do you see the windowpanes beyond the two figures? The young mother in three-quarter profile and the little girl on her knee? That is an old-fashioned sash window such as I had in my bedroom. And can you see there the high-backed chair the mother is sitting in? And the sweet curve of her cheek and her long hair caught back in a bun low on her neck. Very Virginia Woolf, I used to think, much later on of course. And there is the child, her back to us, ringleted, smocked, held safe by her mother's arm which encircles her while holding a book out in front of them both. And with her other hand the mother is pointing at the book. There is something there she wants the little girl to see. A picture, perhaps? A word?

No. I never had children.

You can't see it but the window beyond them is open a little at the bottom and a warm breeze smelling of the sea and the grassy sand dunes is filling the room. And I remember so well the pattern of that blouse she is wearing. Small pretty blue flowers interwoven with tiny green and yellow leaves whose stems I could trace with my fingers as my head leant against her soft breasts and my whole small body soaked up her warmth. And it is at that moment that I first follow with my eyes my mother's pointing finger but then my attention is caught by the words she is saying and so I turn my head to look at her pretty mouth. And as I do that, still within the circle of her arms, I see her lips moving, shaping a sound which escapes and I watch one perfect word fall from her mouth and I reach for it and I catch it. I hold this precious thing up against the sunlight that is streaming in through the window and it catches the light and spills all the colours of the rainbow onto my mother's blouse and my white smock so that I gasp with delight.

I am not crying. When you are as old as I am your eyes water all the time and I think there is a draught coming in from the front door; perhaps the people from the hospital have arrived.

What you can't see in the picture is the large wardrobe which stood against the wall on the other side of the room opposite the window. It had a mirror on the door and when I peered into it I could see a different child.

A little girl with a pale face and a severe haircut. She is wearing one of those prickly woollen jumpers which I hated so much. And there behind me I can see my mother, tidying the room.

She wears a tweed skirt and sensible shoes for the dog-walking which is so important to her. And beyond her the window, not open today but shut and grey with rain.

When the room is tidy she will read to me but, as far as I recall, I never sat on her knee. I think I sat beside her and probably just looked at that picture. It is wonderful, isn't it?

Well, I must go now. It is good of you to listen to an old woman's ramblings. Do you think the doctors at the Memory Clinic would be interested in these memories of mine?

It is a strange thing to me that I can remember everything so clearly and all that is lost is the sound of that word. I've always had such a good memory, particularly for important events like that. Often at night I think I can smell the salt breeze and then I believe I can catch the word again and I hear her voice echoing in my brain but I have never been able to spell it out. It's such a pity.

It was such an important word.

183 MINUTES

As she often said later, if she had not missed the 9:11 to Durham they would never have met. There on the platform in full view of everyone she had burst into tears at the annoyance and worry of it all and then she had had to sit and wait for the 10:15 and to let Jessie know, which was a nuisance. Fortunately she had remembered her phone. But once she was on the train and in her seat she calmed down and when he got on at Leamington Spa she watched him, quietly and unobtrusively, as she always did, having been a people watcher from birth. She had liked the look of him; a touch of Trevor Howard, she thought. And nice luggage. Classy.

They were alone in the first-class carriage that Tuesday morning and he was sitting obliquely from her on the other side of the aisle. She was bent over her crossword puzzle as she watched him eat his croissant, warmed, fortunately, and drink his coffee. She thought he looked sad, pensive at least, while he would confess later that he thought she looked kind. And, as she insisted later, if it had not been that they were sitting in a first-class carriage she would never have spoken to him. Dear Jessie, her favourite, the only one who ever stood up for her, had sent her the fare. And, for his part, the horses had been good to him that week. And he loved travelling first-class. 'I like to be looked after,' he would tell her later, and she could see what he loved, the deference, the layers of courtesy that he had once enjoyed. It recalled the days of wine and roses when he had been up there, top of the tree, top of the top tree, when it came to it. Managing to inspire, control, direct, until . . . until the crash. A lot of people lost too; but that did not really help. 'I took my eye off the ball,' he would say to her one day, 'It was my own stupid fault.' But if she could she would have ensured that he never again went without that level of pleasure.

She had been thinking that he looked sad like her father had been sad; a soft sentimental pensiveness that had turned her heart over when she was a child and probably ever since. And here it was again; a sort of wistfulness that he could not possibly have been aware of. 'They see you coming,' her mother used to say; castigating her father for another investment in a useless project or person.

'Going far?' And he smiled. And he looked again like the businessman he must have been; sharp, a bit of a womaniser perhaps, smooth, untrustworthy. But by then she had glimpsed the sadness and she was curious as well as kind so she surprised herself by not saying, 'Not far,' as she might have done and normally would have done, with a shrug of her shoulders and a glance down at the crossword puzzle. Instead she said, 'Durham. I'm going to visit my granddaughter. Where are you going?'

'York. I'm moving there.'

And suddenly and unexpectedly she felt a lurch of sorrow that he would be so far away. She scanned the crossword. 'You look like a cricketer,' she said, 'May I ask you a word?'

'I'll have a go,' he replied.

'A cricket ball that hits the ground by the batsman's feet.'

'A Yorker.'

And they smiled at each other since it was such a remarkable coincidence. 'You'll soon be a Yorker, then,' she said boldly.

'I live alone,' he added, for no reason at all. 'What about you?'

'I live with my sister.'

And she saw something in his eyes, something unexpected, as he said, 'That's nice.'

She turned her head towards the window, wondering whether she could say, 'I live with my sister, the sadist in a wheelchair.' She told herself often that if she were living as poor Daphne was with a horrible creeping deteriorating disabling illness then she too would have become deceitful and manipulative. Except she did not believe it. She, quite definitely, would have been so horribly embarrassed at the thought of being a burden to anyone that she would never have insisted, as Daph did, on being taken everywhere, on leaking everywhere, on getting drunk and making obscene overtures to everyone around. It made Daphne sound, she knew, according to the fashions of today, like a good sport. A woman who had overturned all the social expectations with which their generation had once been burdened. Those dreadful hushed fifties politenesses; those ghastly drip-dry opinions. But for her part she could never bear the thought of being a nuisance. And she would not have been living with Daphne at all except that Stuart had died and she had been 'left alone' and just as she was savouring the first faint aromas of freedom, the family, that great power, the family formulated the judgement that, 'Now that Stu had died Mum could live with Daph; they would be company for each other.' The fact that the sisters had nothing, but nothing, in common apart from an unfortunate tendency to rosacea had totally escaped the family. In her head she pictured them standing around her, looking down from their Olympian heights of youth, independence, proper jobs, and saying, 'This is our decision, Mum. It will all work out beautifully.'

'But,' she had wanted to say, 'But I am still alive. Let me go. I promise not to be a nuisance. I could . . .' but she had stumbled in her thinking. She had not been fast enough, she had never been fast enough, to outstrip the do-gooders of this world. She was always the one to be trapped by the most boring person in the room. And how uncharitable that was, but she knew, she just knew that there were people somewhere who laughed at each other's jokes, who leant together against the wind along the sea front, who gazed into each other's eyes with such delight that the world changed into something wonderful. She had seen them, the lovers. Stu had always been rather boring too, although she hated to admit it. But her mother had liked him. And she had always longed to please her mother. And then, on her deathbed, her mother had said, 'Look after Daph. You will look after Daphne, won't you?' Daphne was ill by then. But the looking after had always been a part of the agenda. First Stu and then Daphne. And her mother had left the house and everything to Daphne. 'You'll be all right but now that she is ill Daphne needs it. You do understand, don't you?' Naturally, she had understood.

As they talked about the children it had become clear that for a long time now, their roles had been peripheral:

essential, of course, supplying context and depth to the family picture but only in so far as their roles offered a background chiaroscuro to the brightly lit foreground of the younger members. Yet both were also so foolishly fond of the children.

He leant urgently towards her, 'Was it Gibran who said that they are not our children. "You are the bows from which they are sent forth as living arrows." Something like that?'

And she smiled and thought about the psalm that describes children as arrows in the hand of a mighty man. But she did not say this; partly on account of an old habit of secrecy and partly because she did not want to seem competitive. But even more potently because she loved the anticipation of possibly telling him when the time seemed right.

And also she was preoccupied by now by the recognition that something was changing. Their relationship had crystallised in some way and the stuff they had been exchanging about crossword puzzles and inconvenient trains and the weather and where they lived and the children shrank and coalesced into a single point of burning conviction: they understood each other.

And, more than that, as they talked it had become clear that her ideas were echoed by his and his by hers. And then that this echoing had been leading to a degree of amplification, so that she felt her mind widening, broadening, deepening under the impetus of so sweet a series of resonances.

'I can feel your ideas pinging around in my head,' she said, 'And I have so many things I want to say to you.'

And the fact that they understood each other was essential for each had also by now become accustomed to the knowledge that as far as society, and in particular the family, was concerned their lives, their internal, intellectual and emotional, and one could add psychological lives, were non-existent. As though with the advent of wrinkles and a certain uncertainty in their balance went an erasure of all thought, all significance, all hope, all ambition, all (he said to her much later) passion.

Recently she had been plagued by a memory of that time when she was ten and Daph was five. She, who did not have many friends, had a new one. This was a secret friendship. It was an intense, powerful, gorgeous, secret friendship.

Mary lived just a block away in a grand house; her father was the owner of a big brewery. They had only recently moved there and on the first day of the new term she had gone over to the small shy child and played with her during the lunch break. That afternoon Mary's mother had called to invite her to tea. After that, every afternoon she walked around to Mary's house where there was a little side gate that was unlocked just for her. One afternoon, out of the blue, her mother had said, 'I think you should take Daphne with you today. She has no-one to play with.'

'But,' her heart had flipped over in panic, 'but, Mum, we can't climb trees when she's there or . . .' and what she did not say was, our games are secret. Special. There were so many reasons why this would be catastrophic. So many. And then, as she walked along the pavement since she truly did have a kind heart, she looked down at the small head with its pigtails flapping behind it and took her sister's hand. 'It isn't that I don't like playing with you, Daph. It is just that, Mary is a very special friend. I suppose we are used to being alone together.'

And her sister raised her head and in Daphne's eyes she saw for the first time the expression she would become accustomed to seeing all the time. It was triumph. It was an expression of triumph combined with an extraordinarily vindictive malice that made her wince.

'It's not nice, living with my sister,' she said. 'I think of her as the sadist in a wheelchair.'

He did not seem disturbed by this.

'Then I'm sorry,' he said, 'I should not have been so presumptuous.'

'Do you have a sister?'

'I did have. She died a couple of months ago. We own a house together and I had always thought I would stay on there but . . .' his voice trailed away. 'I'm not good at living alone. I'm going today to put a deposit on an apartment in a housing unit. You know, for oldies.'

And there she saw it again, the sadness.

'Have you sold the house?'

'I've had an offer. A good one.'

And now he was the businessman once more. Shrewd, careful, calculating.

'You must miss her a lot.'

'I was married, as you know. Then Fanny's husband died and I got divorced and well, it seemed the obvious thing.'

There was the sound of the trolley approaching.

'Would you like a drink?' he asked.

He moved across the aisle to sit opposite her and bought two small bottles of white wine. It was three for two, he was told, when he asked for two plastic glasses.

'There are just the two of us,' he laughed and looked her straight in the eyes. As he had moved, the light had changed. She could see him more clearly now, as maybe he could see her. She felt shy, embarrassed, telling him so much. It was the old cliché, wasn't it? Strangers on a train.

'To us,' he said as he raised his glass.

'I don't usually talk to strangers on trains,' she said.

'Our eyes are the same colour,' he said after a moment or two, and she could see that they were. 'We're running a few minutes late but it's not long until we get to York.'

She looked at her watch.

'We've been talking for nearly three hours,' she said,

thinking that they really had only just met. And she remembered her tears of frustration that morning.

'I plan to live forever,' he said and she knew, for a fact, that this was the most important truth of his life and that it had always been a secret, shut in his heart, until suddenly, surprising himself as much as he did her, it had been pulled out into the open, for her. Just for her. Because she looked kind. And she had nodded and said, quite confidently, 'I know.' And he relaxed.

'Will you come with me?' he asked and she was not surprised. But Jessie. She could see Jessie's lovely face, its happy welcoming smile changed into something painful, confused, hurt.

'But Jessie will be waiting for me,' she said.

And he could see all the emotions that she had feared for Jessie in her eyes.

'Then I'll come with you,' he said.

And the world fell into place around her. And she turned her face towards the window for she wanted to see if there was a reflection there of the woman she had suddenly become. But in the anonymity of the rushing fields she saw only her body dumped in an alley, at the bottom of a cliff, down a well; and then they flew under a bridge and against the momentary blackness she saw her face again. So that is who I am, she thought. That is who I am now. And, turning quickly away, she said, 'Yes.'

And then, 'But what about your ticket?'

And he held out his hand, palm downwards, moving it sideways as though sweeping away all the unnecessary debris of the past. 'I'll pay the difference,' he smiled, 'Or I'll buy a new ticket for the whole journey.' And he grinned at her and she knew he was telling her that she was worth it. 'Don't worry.'

And when they got to Durham he took her bag and helped her down from the train and then hand in hand they made their way across the unfamiliar platform towards the ticket barrier where she could see Jessie waving and smiling and she waved back thinking her heart might just burst with a sudden joy.

And then, as she used to say later, he had not turned out to be quite what she had expected. But then, she would add, with her need not to be unfair, she wasn't quite what he had expected either. She who had always been a people watcher still watched him but, it occurred to her, now more out of fear than out of love.

Occasionally, when she lay beside him at night, seeing the light from the streetlamps fall across the windowsill, thinking it was as white as moonlight used to be now that the council used LED bulbs in them, she would press herself very gently against his back and think how contentment was a new emotion for her. Sometimes, when they sat together in a pub garden, holding hands, staring over the green fields, she felt completely happy. With him she had even discovered that she had an unexpected capacity for moments of joy that she had never known about, or not since childhood.

It had turned out that there was no sister, just a woman friend who had moved out a few months earlier. 'Were you really going to move to York?' she asked but when he suggested she distrusted him she felt very guilty and never raised the subject again.

'Perfect love casts out fear,' she rebuked herself. 'And now good morrow to our waking souls which watch not one another out of fear,' she recited joyfully, pegging out the washing on the line, deciding to make chilli con carne for supper tonight, one of his favourites.

It never occurred to her to leave. Now that they were married, Stu's pension and her small legacy from her mother were in their joint account. Even if she could have afforded to leave it was not in her nature. Throughout her life she had been taught not to complain, not to make a fuss, not to argue, never to fight back.

It was just over three years later that they found her body in woods near Banbury. As Daphne pointed out, her sister had always been a poor judge of character and the children, of course, were horrified. Only Jessie wept and wept for that late dawning of a naive hope and the courage to reach for it.

THE KISKADEE

Pamela was lying on a lounger on the terrace, stretching her neck to the sun. The heat burnt her eyes and cheeks already washed clean of make-up by her tears and the warmth was unexpectedly wonderful. It was bad for her, of course, bad for her old, ravaged skin but she did not care and she opened herself up to the powerful rays and a little shiver of happiness ran through her. Be careful, she admonished herself, for she had been warned that her moods would be all over the place.

She opened her arms and threw her head back as though offering herself to the sun-god himself and into her tormented mind came a memory of standing like this in the sunlight, a small child naked in the garden at home, the sun warming her all over and her father calling, 'Come here, Queen Mab! Come and make my dreams come true.' For a confusing moment she felt as though she were back there and, as the sun beat down on her closed eyelids, there it was again, quite unbidden.

'Come here, Queen Mab,' her father was saying, 'Give me good dreams,' he said kissing her forehead, 'Make my dreams come true.' How safe she had felt, so safe, so happy. He was sitting in a deckchair and he had pulled her onto his knee and had wrapped her in his strong arms and cupped her head against his chest and she could feel his big hands cradling her small body. Mabel was his name for her when she had been christened. Pamela Mabel Pinkerton. He told her it was from the Latin for loveable, 'amabilis', and she had felt privileged, singled out to be loved.

She was examining the purple and red blooms on the inside of her eyelids and listening to the soothing rattle of the palm fronds in the meandering breeze off the beach when her meditations were intruded upon by the cry of a kiskadee. Squinting against the sunlight she saw the improbably yellow bird against the improbably blue sky. Tourists love the old calypso song about the Yellow Bird but Bermudians know that they are predators, imports from Trinidad, intended to reduce the population of anole lizards but instead preying on the chicks and eggs of smaller indigenous birds. And they have flourished so that, if there is one sound that is constant in Bermuda, it is the incessant three-toned cry of the kiskadee.

Disturbed in this fashion, Pamela now felt disproportionately upset. She could feel the contentment that the sun and the memories had induced in her shrivelling and disappearing in the storm of discomfort that the bird's call was causing her. Indifferent to her agitation, the bird sang on, kis-ka-dee, kis-ka-dee; its raucous cry echoed by another on a neighbouring tree.

Do they call at night, she thought, and then, of course not, all birds roost at night. But she was sure she had heard it last night and she opened her eyes, realising she was dozing off again. Resolutely, she pulled herself to a sitting position on the sun-lounger, reaching for her sunglasses and her sunhat.

Her hat was a flattering wide-brimmed open-weave affair which cast speckles of light upon her face and neck and once she had her sunglasses on as well, she felt grown up again and, indeed, quite restored to her former self.

She looked around at the tables and chairs on the terrace and signalled to a waiter. Having ordered a white wine spritzer and asked for his help in adjusting the back of the lounger she felt almost calm while the birds sang on. But there was nothing mellifluous in these sounds.

By now she could feel the wine making its welcome way into her bloodstream and she looked out beyond the palm trees at the smudgy horizon, rough today like an impressionist painting or a Turner, she thought, as though the two blues bled into each other. And she looked again at the kiskadee. It was perched on the back of a chair a few yards away. It was indeed a handsome bird with a banana-yellow chest and milky brown feathers on its back but its head was quite sinister. Severe horizontal black and white streaks culminated in a long savagely pointed beak. She took a gulp of her drink and looked at her watch. Not long until lunch. She had reserved the table in the restaurant.

But she needed to tidy herself up before then. What a mess she must be.

A couple of tourists wandered past and sat at a table nearby. They were an elderly couple; well, probably just around her age. The man had a nice face. He was not particularly good-looking although he had kept his hair. He was quite stocky and had the expected paunch but he looked, she thought, as though he would be comfortable to be with. As though he would be a warm and happy drunk and affectionate and generous at all times. The woman was quite tall and rather shapely. She had shoulder-length grey hair and two combs to hold it back on either side of her head. Her face was hidden from Pamela as she leant forward and took one of the man's hands and held it to her cheek. He smiled at her and at that point Pamela turned away. The tenderness was almost indecent in its intimacy in what was, after all, a public place.

She looked for the waiter and indicated another spritzer. The breeze was gentle and the palmetto leaves gleamed in the sunlight as though oiled. A bank of orange hibiscus, the butterflies of the flower world, bravely put out their petals for their short life. How to live, thought Pamela, and how to grow old.

This time the waiter brought the drink in a tall glass misted by the moisture in the air. Bermuda was always humid but today she welcomed it. The expansiveness of this balmy sea air was welcome after claustrophobic London. And the service in this place was pretty good. She could afford the best. She had her civil service pension, after all, and she would inherit everything. She had been promised that. She could feel her skin desiccating, shrinking, and she reached for her sunscreen.

She had always been proud of her feet. They were narrow and well-proportioned with a high instep and long toes. A podiatrist had once told her they were 'fairy feet': the kind drawn in children's pictures of flower fairies and princesses. She reached down now to renew the sunscreen, massaging her insteps gently. This familiar process always echoed the day that she had realised that her father was an old man. She could never remember how old she was at the time or how old he was but that was not the important thing. He had been swimming, they all had, and he was standing in the kitchen drying himself, laughing and talking and she had caught sight of his feet and suddenly into her head popped the thought, Daddy is an old man. His feet were veined and lumpy and the toenails thickened and yellow. It was, she said to herself at the time, maybe her first critical response to her father's body but, of course, the real impact was the concomitant fear of his death. She could never bear to think of living in a world without him. Even after she was too big to sit on his knee, she needed to feel his arms around her and to listen to the sound of his voice. Once, when she was a lot older and just into her teens, after she had gone to bed, he had come to say goodnight and had bent over her and kissed her with open lips. Very briefly. So that later she wondered if it had been a mistake. She hadn't minded that. She diligently rubbed sunscreen into her legs and feet. So many people forgot the feet.

The couple were ordering lunch and the kiskadee had disappeared as crowds of fat greedy sparrows clustered around the tables and lined up on the wooden balustrade edging the terrace. The waiters waved them away as though they were flies. She watched the messy dusty little birds as they squabbled and fought among themselves. They too were predators, she reminded herself, occupying nesting-boxes put up for the bluebirds, but they seemed so much more innocent than the kiskadees. Confused rather than cruel.

Pamela had reserved a table in the restaurant which would be air-conditioned with white tablecloths and nice china and proper knives and forks. These things had come to matter to her as she got older. And she had been given a taste for luxury by her father. He had liked her to enjoy good things.

Sometimes, she used to travel with him on his lecture tours. They had invariably been put up in good hotels, often in adjoining rooms, since she had always had a tendency to nightmares and he had worried about this a great deal. It was not uncommon for her to wake up, her heart racing with a thudding sound that she had thought, as a child, was the sound of the nightmare running away. Then she would find herself almost too terrified to move but she would force herself out of bed and run into her father's room and hide there under the sheets, consoled by the presence of his large warm body.

Waking up one morning and looking out of the window

and seeing sunshine, sea and mountains, she had felt so excited that she had run down the corridor and knocked on the door. He was busy making tea for the two of them and he had said, 'Come in, my dear. We'll have a treat.' So they sat in his bed, side by side against the big pillows while they drank the tea and he gave her a sip of brandy from his hip flask and lit a cigarette for her. 'After all, if it is not me, darling, it will be someone else.'

It was one of her best memories. She must have been no more than fourteen but it felt so grown up, to watch the morning sunlight creep across the floor from the window which opened onto a balcony above the grand landscaped gardens while the brandy made her gasp and she drew on her cigarette and they blew smoke rings together. She had felt so utterly happy.

Pamela had finished her spritzer and looked again at her watch. Slabs of pale grey cloud lay above the horizon. A plane carved a white line up the sky. She glanced at the couple beside her. She wanted to be able to say, 'Isn't that lovely?' Loneliness gaped like a great echoing abyss beneath her.

*

Her father had been so persistent in his dreams for her and she had so wanted to make these dreams come true but she had failed to find a husband that matched his expectation. There had been Rob, in her first year; clever like her father. He had got her drunk on gin and waltzed with her to *La Traviata* and she knew she could have loved and adored him forever. But her father had thought their engagement was a bit sudden and suggested she break it off and focus on her studies.

She was jerked out of sleep as her head fell forward toward her chest and the kiskadee blasted her again with his harsh cry. God, she was dopey this morning. It was because she hadn't slept much last night. Despite the pills. She stared at the bird. He was undoubtedly handsome in a primary colour sort of way. He turned his head and his sinister profile was silhouetted against the sky. She had been told once that they could stab chicks in the nest with their beaks and she shivered to think of it. Could it be true? And a shadow of a dream passed over her mind from last night. Something inescapable, irresistible and infinitely horrifying would not take no for an answer. Persistent, demonic, like a toad squatting on the

stair or a hobgoblin crouching on your chest it would leave
you paralysed, unable to move, unable to speak. The crazy
irrationality of dreams! After she had left home and settled
in at university it was on account of her night terrors, which
her friends had worried about, that she had been offered some
counselling. For trauma, apparently. That was what the doctor
had said and the six sessions were compulsory. Looking back,
she wondered whether she had experienced even the counsellor as a large predatory bird. Seemingly caring, in reality
probing, refusing to take no for an answer.

'I have had a very happy childhood. In fact, I have
probably been quite spoilt.'

'But what was it like at home? How did your parents
get on?'

And there was her mother's face, baffled, confused, sad.
'Your father is very manipulative.'

She had not intended to tell the counsellor that but it
had slipped out.

'Could your mother have been right?'

'My father was a wonderful man. Everyone loved and
admired him.'

'How would you feel if I suggested that your father might have been a predator?'

'What do you mean, a predator?'

'That he took advantage of you. That he abused you.'

Of course, she left when the six sessions were up.

The couple at the nearby table had eaten their hamburgers with what looked like childish delight, and he had leant over to wipe a smear of ketchup from the side of her mouth with his finger, which he then licked.

Pamela beckoned to the waiter and asked for a glass of Sauvignon Blanc. It would be good here. Her father had always wanted her to have the best. While she waited she looked across the terrace at the leaves of the palmettos shining against the multi-shaded blueness of the sea. The shaggy silhouette of a cedar tree rose high above the shrubs by the shoreline. The white roofs of guest cottages could be seen below the terrace and on the ridge of one was the kiskadee. He never stopped. She really hated him. The call was relentless, kis-ka-dee. kis-ka-dee.

Once when she had been quite small her father had taken her to visit her grandmother in Ireland. They had shared the only guest bedroom up in the attic and he would cuddle her at night, his big body enfolding hers, like a little bud, he said. And he had breathed into her neck and made her giggle. My little Mabel, he would say. My own little dreamer.

He had told her about Queen Mab in *Romeo and Juliet* and said that 'Dreamers dream things true when Queen Mab has been with you.'

'You are with me. You are my dreamer,' he would say. 'My dreamer of dreams. Tell me what you see. Will I be happy? Will you?' and, of course, she would have told him anything, anything at all. For seeing the expression of delight on his face was the best, the very best thing in the world.

It was Terry who had distrusted her father. Terry had played the piano, as her father did, and he was clever and wise and loved her deeply, but her father had not really taken to him. It was never entirely clear why although her mother had said that her father was a snob. They had hitch-hiked to Athens during their last summer and she had loved it and him and after they graduated he said they should go and live in Greece and just see what happened. As she sipped her Sauvignon Blanc she remembered the first taste of Ouzo in a little bar overlooking the harbour and how she had loved, had just loved, okra.

Kis-ka-dee, sang the bird. Predator. Kis-ka-dee. Predator. Kis-ka-dee. Kis-ka-dee. She thought she might scream.

It was nearly time for lunch. She shouldn't spend so much time with her memories. They stirred things up and made her sad. If she had tried to put this sadness into words she might have said, 'Daddy, what is it you have never forgiven me for?' Could it have been that one night after her mother had died when his white skin had been flabby and even spongy to touch and possibly he had sensed her repulsion. But as she herself got older, and fatter, and wrinkled, she had begun to wonder whether it was simply that she had grown up and was no longer the child she had been. It was a long time since she had sensed that she was able to please him. Of being his dreamer. His little Mabel.

Not long ago, her father had written her a letter in which he had said, 'You have been the love of my life.' She had kept the letter of course. It was hidden safely in the little escritoire she had inherited from her mother. It was not a small thing, she said to herself, to have been loved like that.

The waiter came over to her.

'Your table is ready, Miss Pinkerton. And Sir Toby is already there.'

And she hadn't tidied herself at all. She knew she looked a complete mess. Why had she allowed herself to be waylaid by all these memories? She cast one more glance at the kiskadee who sang on, impervious to her distress. Well there was nothing for it. Being late was always unforgivable.

She crossed the terrace, a little unsteadily, an elderly, overweight woman with a sad face but as she walked towards the table the old excitement began to build again.

He would be there.
He would be there.

'Daddy,' she said.

And there he was and she felt her heart lift, just as it always had done.

THE QUESTION

PAIN EVERYWHERE. Pain swamping my body, crawling into my head, down my arms and legs, pain so that I hesitated to open my eyes in case that hurt too. A steady hand slides under my head at the back and carefully raises it and something smooth is pushed into my dry mouth and I swallow the liquid. My head is laid down again. In a heartbeat, a sweet, delicious languor sweeps through me. I could have wept with relief. I open my eyes and silhouetted there against the harsh white lights of the ceiling is a face. A man's face. Smooth, even-featured, kindly, smiling, 'Hello, Mrs Simpson. I'm your nurse today. My name is Donny. What would you like me to call you?'

Floating in a pain-free universe I smile back. 'Call me Anne.'

'You've had a fall. A bad fall. You've injured your back and we need to do some tests.'

I nodded, without pain.

'Sure,' and I closed my eyes again.

Obviously, my recollections of that brief encounter must be considered unreliable due to the pain, the drugs, and possibly my age. However, I do clearly remember thinking, as I drifted away, that I had just seen the face of an omnipotent, benevolent God and also that he looked remarkably familiar.

I next remember the pain edging its way back into my consciousness as I examined the usual bland hospital ceiling composed of those squares of what look like soundproofing material and maybe are. To muffle the cries, I guess. I found that I was lying on a bed in what seemed to be a large ward but as the pain was coming back I could not easily raise my head to see. I traced my memories backwards to work out why I was here. I had been in the kitchen in my pyjamas waiting for the kettle to boil when I heard the doorbell. I raced to open it but the courier had reached the pavement. I yelled and started to run down the steps but they were icy and my bare foot slipped and I fell heavily down to the bottom. I thought I was going to die. I must have winded myself.

'Hello, Anne. How is the pain?'

'Coming back.'

'I thought so.'

Once again the kindly hand and once again the elixir.

'Is it morphine?'

'Yes. Do you remember what happened?'

I told him. But only half my mind was working on this problem; the other half was dealing with the conviction that I knew Donny's face. After a while I closed my eyes again. I leafed through a thick file of memories. Donny. But maybe not his name then? And where was he? Where was I? And how long ago. Ah ha! Another page or rather another chapter and there he was. Gordon. Gordon something. Of course. The unforgettable Gordon.

And I slipped away again but not without a small sense of anxiety, an uncertain awareness of my own failure, a ripple of unease that had pushed its way into my consciousness before being erased by the magic of the opioid.

When I woke up again there was a plate with two sandwiches on it on the tray next to my bed and a Thermos of water. Also a cold cup of coffee. Donny was taking my blood pressure again.

'This is coming down nicely.'

'But, am I all right?'

'We've done every test and scan that we should and we're just waiting for a couple more results. But you have not had a stroke or a heart attack. We can see you have compressed your ninth and tenth thoracic vertebrae and you're going to be in some pain over the next few weeks but that should pass and otherwise you are fine. We'll send a letter to your GP. Do we need to send occupational health round to your house?'

'God, no. I just need to not race out barefoot after couriers on icy mornings.'

'You're lucky, Anne. You could have done a lot more damage.' I peered into his benign, generous features, looking for any sign of recognition. My surname would have been different. I had used my unmarried name at work.

'I'll come back and check on you shortly. And I'll make sure you have another cup of coffee.'

It was rather pleasant lying there in the afterglow of the morphine, completely relaxed, out of pain, no responsibilities, the ward full of those small indistinguishable sounds that indicate the presence of other people doing useful work.

Now able to be propped up, I ate two cheese sandwiches and drank my coffee while I revisited my memories.

It was the third meeting of three. We were in the Outpatients Department of the Psychotherapy Services section of the local psychiatric hospital and it was my job then as psychiatric registrar to assess patients for the therapy group programme we offered. We were sitting in my consulting room in the two armchairs strategically placed there for the purpose. I was young but he was even younger; a good-looking boy, blond, I think, with a narrow face and an impish smile when he was at ease. But now he is tense and tearful. And resolute. Determined to say what he felt had to be said.

'I can't believe I am saying this but, I had sex with my own mother.'

People in my line of work are very clear that the consulting room is not a confessional. Nobody need say more than they want. But all those years ago Gordon clearly felt he needed to be absolved of his sin and being that day in the role of a secular priest it was my job to make this happen.

He had seemed to be relieved that I had neither collapsed nor screamed nor called the police.

'You see,' he said, 'It was all so . . . unexpected.'

'Of course.'

'I had decided to look for my birth mother,' he said. 'I was given an address, I wrote, a proper letter, just saying I'd like to meet, and she telephoned me. That was it. She sounded kind, on the phone. Kind, and as though she was really pleased to think I had thought of her. It probably helped that I was able to tell her that I had been very well cared for in my adoptive home.'

He sat back in the chair at that point, stretching out his legs as he expanded into a chatty, conversational mode. I guessed that it was an enormous relief to be able to tell this story at last and, after all, I had been trained to be a good listener. The story spilt out of him. His mother was in the sixth form when she got pregnant and he had been adopted as soon as he was born by a kind and supportive middle-aged couple with no children. He had excelled at school and moved into sciences. Went to a university up north to study engineering. Got a good degree but three years later found himself with a steady job, no girlfriend, lonely and bored to death and possibly depressed. 'I just spent all day looking at a computer screen,' he said.

'You think you might have been depressed?'

A long silence. 'As I grew older I missed my mum, you see. I can't explain it. I just wanted to see her. I had this idea that mothers have a special relationship with their sons. My adoptive mother was lovely, but she was more like a grandmother than a mother. Anyway, my parents were fine with it. So after my mother rang me, I caught a train up to Edinburgh. It was some way and I had decided to spend the night there. She had given me the address of a pub where we could meet and I found a B&B, checked in. I was so nervous. We had agreed on six o'clock. I was there early, I always am, early for everything. Got there with my newspaper and waited in a corner. She ran in just after six, looked around, and saw me. She smiled as though she recognised me. She was really beautiful. You must remember my idea of a mother was my adoptive mother who was almost old when she got me. My own mother was not yet forty then with a sweet, pretty, kind face and long brown hair. We were at ease from the start. Of course, we covered everything. My dad had been a school friend. "Very good at Maths," she emphasised. She said I looked like him. I asked her if she had ever had a name for me. It had always been a bit of a bugbear as I hate the name Gordon. She shook her head.

"'I thought it wouldn't be fair, to you or to me. So I called you Baby. But," and her eyes filled with tears, "I loved you, Baby. I loved you more than anything in the whole world. I think I still do." And she choked up and I started crying too and I tried to put my arms around her to comfort her and she was doing the same and by now we were standing and holding each other and I kissed her wet cheek and she moved her head and by mistake our mouths met and . . . we kissed. By now we felt that we were being stared at, so we walked out to get some privacy. We had a lot more to talk about. We ended up at the B&B.' Now he looked at me through the tears. 'I felt so ashamed.'

'You needn't have felt ashamed,' I said.

He smiled with relief. 'That's kind of what she said. That we mustn't feel bad. "It's OK. Promise me you won't worry about this," she said. "It is all OK." And she was soothing me while I was worried about her. Anyway, eventually she left. She had a life to return to. Teenage kids, a job, a home, a husband, a life. And that's when I decided to make a new life for myself. In a way, I felt I owed it to her.' He paused. 'You see, she really loved me.'

A ward orderly slid a menu card onto the table beside me. I have always been quite fond of institutional food and I allowed myself to toy with the idea of spending the rest of my life here. It was peaceful, undemanding, anonymous. Except, there was after all a possibility that Donny was being as discreet as I was, in which case the idea of anonymity was shot. I wondered again how much of our shared past might be in his mind today. Features do not change much no matter how greatly the ageing process marks a face. And he was clearly an observant person. He would be no good as a nurse if he were not. He could make his patients feel that he was a safe pair of hands. Had I once had that quality too? He had certainly trusted me. Entrusted himself to me. When we met he had told no-one else the big secret. I believed that. Love is a complicated emotion. I tried to recall what Dylan Thomas, who understood more than most, had said. A woman in bed with a man is mother, sister, daughter, lover all in one? Was that it?

Gordon had explained that he had some savings by then since he had had no life to spend his money on and he had decided he wanted to work with people. In the last six months he had moved south and by the time I met him he was about to start training as a nurse at the local hospital.

Then, he had decided, he needed to find some therapy. And so here he was, in front of me.

'What was your mother's job?' I asked.

He gave me a triumphant smile. 'She was a nurse.'

Gordon joined my therapy group. It met twice a week, Tuesdays and Fridays. He was an excellent member, interested, compassionate, intelligent, committed. And early for every session. He stayed in the group for nearly five years. He achieved a lot and he successfully completed his nurse training and found a girlfriend. She was a junior doctor. Two medics. The last I knew they were thinking of emigrating to New Zealand. Were they still together? Was he happy? But that was not the question that was burning in my mind. It was another question that I had decided I should never ask.

When the subject of his birth mother had come up in the group, as it was bound to, 'I never bothered,' he said. 'I had nothing to say to her.' However, shortly before he was due to leave the group, he returned to the subject. 'Before I leave, I want to tell you something. I wasn't entirely honest about my mum. To be truthful, I was ashamed.'

I had been wondering about this moment for a long time.

'The thing is, I had always had this dream. About a mother who fell in love with me, as a baby, I mean, you know, like the books say. That mothers fall in love with their babies. That sort of thing. It was a dream, of course, only a dream, but so strong. I could not let go of it. So, after I started work, I did track her down. There's a bit of a story to it. I had arranged to meet her in a pub. I caught the train up to Edinburgh where she was then and went to the pub she had named. I got there early, of course. Found a table, sat down with my paper. There was a very attractive woman at the bar. Young. Long brown hair. Really pretty. She was a bit tipsy. She was drinking with this guy and laughing and after a while I heard her say her adopted son was on his way up to see her. And I looked up, without meaning to, and saw her sort of smirk at this chap. "He's got a proper job, he's loaded." It made me feel sick. In fact even now,' and he reached for the box of tissues, 'I can't bear to think of that moment. Dreams. Every adopted child is full of them. And she was just . . .' he didn't finish the sentence. 'I left without speaking to her.'

Of course, the group rallied around, expressing sympathy, support, understanding.

'Anne, how are you feeling?'

'Much better, thanks, Donny.'

'Results are all back. No serious problems. Would you like to go home tonight?'

'Can I take some morphine with me?'

He shook his head. 'You could stay overnight if you wanted.'

But I knew that if I were admitted they would take me up to some other ward where there would be no Donny. And anyway, it must be nearly the end of his shift.

'I think I'll go home.'

'I can give you painkillers, Anne. And I can get an ambulance car to take you home. Is there anyone there to keep an eye on you? Could we give them a call?'

In the end they called my neighbour Simon and he came to get me bringing one of Sarah's coats and some flip-flops. A porter wheeled me down to reception where Simon was waiting.

'You don't look too bad,' he said.

'It's the morphine,' I said. 'Knocks years off your age.'

And so I re-entered my ordinary life.

But just before I left the ward, as I was sitting in the wheelchair, clutching my paper bag of painkillers, there was Donny, walking towards me, smiling his wonderful smile.

'Goodbye, Anne. Please be careful where you put your feet in future.'

'Goodbye, Donny. And thank you for everything. Thank you for looking after me so well.'

Our eyes met as he shook my hand. Did he murmur something about being looked after? Did he know who I was? Were we both simply observing our professional boundaries? One thing I was certain about was that I would never ask that critical question. I am sure I know the answer anyway.

ON BEING ALONE

H ER FINE WHITE HAIR stood out around her head like a gauzy halo framing the sunburnt face. A lifetime of African sunshine had left so many creases in her skin that she looked as though her tiny body had been only partially inflated and even the back of her skinny neck was creased. I had looked for that when she limped out onto the veranda where I had been waiting while my father examined her in her bedroom. She smiled at me then and said, 'She's getting big, Doctor,' while she bent over a large wicker chair and then sort of collapsed sideways into it. From deep within the wrinkled eyelids two pale green eyes peered out at me as she bent forward to light her cigarette to the flame my father held out for her. She inhaled deeply, throwing her head back and then puffing the smoke upwards.

'Sit down, child. Sit down,' and she waved her free hand towards me. My father was sitting in the wicker chair opposite hers and that left the swing seat for me. This was as big as a small sofa and full of soft cushions and suspended by two chains from a metal frame. I loved sitting there but felt an irresistible urge to swing on it which I thought I was probably not meant to do. I had tried it out while I had been waiting. I often accompanied my father when he was on call and had to visit his patients in their homes but I knew I had to be on my best behaviour. This was not hard for me. I was by inclination an obedient child and I relished the approval I could earn in this way.

'We'll have some coffee. And you'd like a cool drink.'

I nodded. 'Yes, please.'

Ma Lindsey's ancestors had been born in Ireland. She was the seventh child of a seventh child and she was born in a caul, and that made her a soothsayer, my father had told me.

I had known about the creases in the back of her neck from my mother who had said to my father, 'You know even the back of her neck is creased, Jim. And she smokes so much. She looks somehow, smoked, like a kipper.' And then they had laughed together, which I was glad to see, and he said, 'Like a kipper! Oh Nora, that is brilliant. She is, she is as smoked as a kipper!'

I had never eaten a kipper and was not sure what a kipper was except that it was a fish and people had them for breakfast back home in England. Of course, I had read about them. All my books were about people 'back home'. England. Or Scotland or Ireland. The places we came from and to which we would return one day. However, Ma Lindsey's great-grandparents had emigrated to Africa years and years ago and she would never leave. 'She will die here,' I had heard my father say.

So I looked with added interest at the old woman as her cigarette smoke curled around her like a snake and at her dried-up hands and face and sniffed to see if she smelt like a fish too. Her chickens scratched the dry earth around the veranda where we sat and I watched them through the wire netting. One looked up at me holding its head to the side and eyeing me as though it understood everything I was thinking. Did Ma Lindsey talk to them? My father had told me she was a wise woman and could understand animals, and the stars, and she could tell the future and read people's palms. I was handed a glass of orange squash with a straw. My mother, I knew, would worry about the water. We only drank boiled water at home. My father, however, seemed to be untroubled so I sipped it warily. It was too strong. In fact, I began to wonder if it was diluted at all.

It was peaceful sitting there, swinging ever so slightly, sipping through the straw, watching my father and Ma Lindsey smoking and chatting about the weather. This was October, getting towards the end of the dry season, what my father called 'the suicide month' as tensions on the mine between the managers and the miners grew and even families began to fight and men drank too much and beat their wives and children. Only when the storms came would the air be cleared as the rain poured down turning the red earth into streams of swirling red mud and lightning cracked overhead and great thunderheads smashed together and the rain beat down on the corrugated iron rooves of our bungalows with a sound like horses' hooves. A mangy old dog appeared and walked through the cluster of chickens who ignored it. I heard Ma Lindsey say my name.

'Come here, child.'

I climbed down off the swing seat and put my drink down on a small table made out of an elephant's foot. She took my left hand in hers and turned it over and peered down at the palm.

'Aagh, look at this, Doctor. You've got a clever girl here.' She stroked my palm with her other hand which felt like a soft warm paw and ran a nail down one of the lines on my palm. It was almost but not quite painful but I did not draw my hand away for I had learnt not to show when things hurt. She spoke with a thick Afrikaans accent, like the one that would characterise my voice when I and my parents would finally return home. Then these guttural tones and flattened, shortened vowels identified me as a foreigner and I am still sometimes told by very perceptive people that there is a recognisable echo of this in my voice. This pleases me for I like to know that the traces of our past are irreversibly woven into our current lives and are there for those who can, to see.

'You'll go far, my girl, you'll travel. Travel a lot. A lot of car journeys, but you'll be safe on the roads. I see two men, one fair, one dark. Both important. You'll have a long life, and a good one. You'll be successful. But you'll die alone. Much loved, you'll be much loved, plenty of people to love you, but you'll die alone.'

The green eyes twinkled at me through the creases of her lids and her mouth widened in a grin so that I could see her few tobacco-brown teeth. 'But that won't trouble you much, will it? You're a brave girl and we're all alone in the end, aren't we, Doctor?'

My father, who was a bit of a philosopher, nodded. 'We're all alone in the end.'

My father's car was a bright green Hudson Rambler: one of those enormous American cars like a Cadillac in which I would learn to drive one day when I was sixteen. When that time came I often drove too fast on the long, empty roads between the townships for had Ma Lindsey not told me that I would be safe on the roads?

From her place it was about eight miles back to the township down the single strip of tarmac which represented the Great North Road. On either side were wide stretches of red earth and beyond these lay the African bush, the tangle of low trees and grasses and dambos and anthills and animals and snakes that I had been taught never to venture into alone.

As we travelled, I reflected that throughout my life I had been warned that being alone could be risky. I was only allowed to ride my pony in the bush with my father and I had to stay close to him and always be aware that at any moment our horses could be spooked by a snake.

'Is Ma Lindsey very wise?' I asked as we munched on one of the chocolate bars he always had stored in the glove compartment.

'Yes, but she has some pretty wild ideas too.' My father always talked to me as though I were an adult. I liked that. It made me feel clever and grown up but when I got home I told my mother that Ma Lindsey had said I would die alone.

'Much loved but alone,' was what she said.

As I knew would happen my mother was then cross with

my father. 'How could you let that crazy old woman tell the child things like that?'

'Don't worry,' said my father soothingly, 'She'll forget all about it.' But my father who was very clever and philosophical and took me out in the garden at night to look at the Southern Cross through his telescope and treated me as an adult understood me less well than my mother who said, 'No she won't, Jim. It is the kind of thing she will remember all her life.'

And she was right, as she usually was. I believed I had been ascribed a certain fate and I needed to understand what this meant. I had always known it was important to stay alive, if only for the sake of my parents, and being the diligent little philosopher I had been brought up to be, I began to ponder on the meaning of being alone. There was a rich seam to mine here, a fault line running through my character, for I am, by nature, solitary. What that effectively means in practice is that a joy shared is a joy halved and a trouble shared is a trouble doubled. And if I look back now through all the years of the long life that Ma Lindsey had accurately promised me I can see that I was always calibrating the relative merits of being alone or not. As a child I already knew that I needed, craved, bathed myself in solitude. Being alone was my best place. As I grew through my teens I began to understand it better. I narrowed it down to a fear of belonging. Belonging to me meant losing some-thing, not gaining anything. Losing individuality, losing, dare I say, specialness. I was a secretive and isolated child and I feared being identified with any other child as some people might fear the plague. Did I sense some contagion in intimacy with others? Yes, I think so. I reflected long and hard on the implications of my tragic destiny.

And then, what was being alone? Being the other side of a room? The other side of a wall? The other side of a country? Of a continent? I read Larkin's 'Best Society' and quoted the last lines to myself with a tremor of recognition.

When I was eighteen my father's contract came to an end and we returned to England. Once there I found a curious reversal took place. Although I had spent all my conscious life longing to return to the romantic image of foggy, lamplit pavements which for me characterised London, once there I began to feel a kind of nostalgia for my part of Africa.

'What's it like?' I was asked and I stumbled for words to describe it. I tried to imagine Ma Lindsey in Surrey and failed.

Then I went off to university. This was the first time I had left home and everyone told me I would feel lonely. However, I doubted that would be the case. I had, of course, by this stage trodden the well-worn intellectual paths around the question of aloneness versus loneliness. I was not concerned. I knew that fortune tellers did not really exist. I was looking forward to proving that I was still a clever girl and then there were the boyfriends, of whom there were suddenly quite a lot. I tried to work out whether sharing a drink or indeed a bed made one more or less alone and concluded that both situations were irrelevant. Aloneness was something one carried within oneself and there was no getting away from it. So, my reassessment of Ma Lindsey continued and I decided that she might have been crazy but she had seen something in my palm that was true.

From time to time I still wondered how to identify the two men she had promised would be part of my fate. As it happened, while I was at university, I met them both and I married the fair one soon after I graduated. My father and mother had by then responded to a call from the Red Cross for medical assessors in a war-torn country and I was suddenly in need of a home. My intellectual competence had not equipped me for managing my own affairs after all and a home was on offer and so I married the fair boy although I was fervently but secretly yearning body and soul for his best friend. Yes, he was the dark one. Fortunately, as in the best fairy tales, the fair one was also kind, honourable and trustworthy. We all know there is a common assumption that marriage brings companionship although we all also quote Chekhov along the lines of, 'if you fear loneliness, never marry'. I was alone in my marriage and it suited me. Or I thought it did. We had two wonderful children and gave dinner parties and joined clubs and played tennis and had friends around to play Monopoly. We looked like a couple but I was never there. We lived alongside each other for eighteen years at which point we realised there were better ways to live and we split up, with honour and without too much acrimony. I collapsed back into a solitary way of life with gratitude. The former best friend, who had apparently not loved me when it mattered, came calling and we established a distant but passionate sexual conspiracy during which my bodily yearnings were fully satisfied although I believe my soul remained neglected.

During this time I also downsized, found a new home and put a lot of energy into my career which, surprisingly, flourished. I wrote historical novels. I was not proud of them but the proceeds paid the bills. A reviewer called the first one, 'staid but pleasing' and the fourth novel was described as 'formulaic'. It stung but they were right. I had hit on a formula that worked. I would have preferred, of course, to have written a *Mrs Dalloway* for our times. But when I was alone with the screen in front of me my courage failed. And yes, I have asked myself since then whether this was the literary version of being afraid to go into the bush alone? Maybe it was. However, I did not explore that question any further and I proved very successful at being self-sufficient during those years. An onlooker would have said I was flourishing. Could I be described as being alone? Definitely. Was I worried? No. Ma Lindsey's green eyes lurked at the back of my mind although I looked back at the credulous little girl I had been with a degree of fondness and disbelief. But everything was about to change again.

I had bought a small house on the outskirts of the city in an area that possessed the convenience of a suburb and the charm of a village. My house stood on the top of a hill and there was a long row of similar houses all down the street to a little bridge across the river with a view of the water-meadows beyond. One day my eldest granddaughter asked if she could come and live with me as she had a place at a local sixth-form college. I have always believed that the signs of successful mothering are that the children can leave home but, my granddaughter wanting to move in with me, well, that was an unexpected gift. We were in the car one day, I was driving her back to the bus station after a visit, when she said, 'Granny, can I come and live with you?' And I, without hesitation, heard myself say, 'Yes.' It was so simple. Yes. No questions, just yes. From my heart. For two years she lived with me and I with her. There was all the usual teenage stuff. Driving to parties, collecting at midnight, meeting friends, hosting boyfriends, providing money. Worrying. Dropping her off at her insistence in what seemed to me undesirable neighbourhoods, asking her if she did not want to take a coat on a cold November evening. Lying awake, listening for the front door. Trying not to intrude. Finding out what she liked to eat. Once I cooked her lamb's liver. Never again. Once she made me a card for Mother's Day. I still have it. She wrote inside, 'Because you look after me like a mother'. I was in my late sixties by then and I look back on those times with such fondness. I believe we were a unit. I cried when she left but she never looked back. This is how it goes. The love I gave her she will hand on. It trickles down, not up. That is how it should be. And I was arrogant enough to think that I had this being alone stuff sorted. Until the strangest thing happened.

It was October again and that year it stole some of March's thunder and came in like the proverbial lion. And, like a lion, it terrorised the village and everybody felt scared and overwhelmed and talked about little else. Its winds roared around us, whipping the still leafy strands of the willows along the river into a frenzy as though they were long fronds of seaweed beneath breaking waves; it tore some trees down and leapt upon the storm clouds, crushing the rain out of them so that oceans of water fell onto the land, already wet from September's incessant drizzle. The rivers filled up and some flooded their banks. Our river rose above the level of the bridge and although the arch in the centre of the bridge remained just clear of the water level the road either side of it was impassable. The last cottage in the row now had several feet of water surging through it as the swollen river lapped at the foot of the lane. I had seen the woman who lived there when she was working in our local charity shop. I walked down while she was struggling with the help of some of her neighbours to replace the useless sandbags and asked if she would like to move in with me until her home was habitable again.

She was a skinny, nervous woman, with very dark brown eyes and a thin anxious face, rather bird-like in many ways, like the birds she looked for and fed every day. She fed them and I fed her. I take after my mother's side of the family. Plump people, thick-necked and double-chinned, shrinking in height into a round ball with age; they were robust in many ways, but needed to be pampered. She was like a small bird, she brought out in me all those feelings that are nurtured within children when they carry around a doll or a teddy bear, for what else is that caretaking attitude but a determination to feel large and powerful as you lend your larger size and greater strength to care for these dependent creatures. It helps that the toys are immobile without us and can be discarded at a whim, unlike our later human dependents, although to my shame I had, in the course of my life, cherished my ability to discard people, lovers, friends, colleagues, when in my eyes they had outlived their usefulness or their desirability. Hence, perhaps, the inevitability of dying alone but Miriam brought out something different in me. By calming her I felt my own calmness. She began to feel like a part of me.

My house has two bedrooms and a bathroom upstairs and a little junk room. She moved in for an indeterminate time, a few weeks or months, I suggested, until her house could be dried out and refurbished. She spent a lot of time down there as the water receded and she got it professionally tanked and painted. She was a passionate gardener and she rescued many of her best plants and brought them up the hill to my garden.

'You don't mind, do you? I'll take them back when everything is back to normal.' Naturally, I didn't mind.

We rapidly developed a new normal. We shared the bathroom. She was extremely orderly and I grew quite fond of the presence of the extra toothbrush and the tidily folded towel on the towel rail. She helped me discover an interest in birdwatching and we went on a nature weekend to the Highlands and we liked it so much we decided to plan another. It was unduly expensive to reserve and pay for two single rooms so eventually we decided, I forget when, to share a room when we travelled. By this time her house was in excellent condition and we decided it would be simpler to let it. Very soon it was providing us with a good income. As the months went by I found a new happiness in the knowledge of her proximity and in the confidence of her presence at night and it became clear to both of us that Miriam and her plants were here to stay. She was a good cook and after finishing the day's writing I soon got into the habit of looking forward to sitting down with a glass of wine, or sometimes a gin and tonic, to talk over the day. Often we would go out into the garden and she might show me a sick plant, or a new one, and I would let her know how the latest chapter was progressing. Then, perhaps, in winter, a steak and kidney pie or a roast chicken and some vegetables from the garden. In the summer she made lovely salads. I would look at her and wonder what it was that had drawn me to her. She was no beauty. Her dark hair hung untidily across her thin face like a schoolgirl's but I loved the seriousness of her expressions, the slight indentations between her eyebrows which never went away even when she was smiling. When we lay together at night I found such peace in holding her twitching, restless body in my arms. I smoothed her hair and murmured to her as she fell asleep. And so three years passed. How happy I was. How happy we were. Now and again, I asked myself if I was alone. Company I had long ago disqualified as a measure of aloneness for I had learned in the past that even sexual intimacy did not banish aloneness. And I was proud by now of my capacity to carry my essential aloneness everywhere. Of course I will die alone, I said to myself, after all I have lived alone all my life. And I felt again the soft warm touch of that wrinkled little hand and the sharp pain of Ma Lindsey's nail as she drew it across my palm.

And then the weekend came when Miriam told me that she felt she had to go and visit her sister. They were not close, she had hardly seen her for many years, but her sister was very ill. She lived in Inverness. Miriam had heard from a nephew that she was close to death. She had asked to see Miriam. My first impulse was annoyance. What had we to do with them? What had she to do with us? However, reason quickly intervened and I said, with as good grace as possible, 'Of course you must go, Miriam. I'll be fine here for a few days.'

'Are you sure?' she asked. I looked at her. The two indentations deeper than ever. 'I don't really want to leave you.'

And as I looked at her I wanted to scream, 'No! No! Please don't go! Don't leave me! I'll die without you!' But I had never ever, in my whole life, said there was anything I could not manage. I could survive anything, even if it hurt. I had never begged for anything in my life. I simply did not plead. Hesitantly, she looked away and said, softly, 'You could come too, if you wanted.'

But that was the last thing I wanted. I could imagine an unfortunate scenario of family wailings and embarrassing intimacies.

'You go,' I said. 'For God's sake, I'll be fine.'

As I watched her get into the taxi for the station I felt a terrible sense of doom again.

'I'll be back soon. If you need me sooner just ring.'

'I will.'

She had gone for four days and three nights and I would be alone again except for the cat. I have not yet mentioned the cat who has a significant part to play in this last chapter of my life. When she had scrambled up the hill from the flooded house Miriam had brought an armful of cat with her. Susie was an enormous cat. Furry, fluffy, tufted all over, with large, pointed ears and a scornful demeanour. She had been rescued from the river by Miriam. Advertising brought no response. So she stayed. She showed no interest in the birds which Miriam took as a sign of her superior intelligence.

That first evening Miriam rang to say she had arrived safely. It was all pretty grim but her nephew was grateful to her for being there. She was not sure that her sister had recognised her but she was glad to have come. My heart raced. I longed for her to return. I was beginning to recognise that in truth I had never ever, in my whole life, been alone. To be alone you need to need someone who is absent. The need, the belonging was what did it. You had to admit that you depended on another. You needed to need that other like life itself. I am an old woman and evidently a rather foolish one since this was a new thing for me. As I went to bed that first night I thought, when Miriam comes back I must tell her this. And I must never, ever let her go away without me again. Was this why Ma Lindsey had twinkled at me that afternoon so long ago? Had she seen something I had no idea of at all? She had said I would be brave. Well I was trying to be brave but I had never known such unhappiness and I cried like the child I once was and buried my head in the pillow. The second night I managed better. When she called I told her everything was OK but that there was a terrible storm blowing up. There was a warning of ice. I put Susie's supper out, as per instructions, but she was not there. Normally she would hang about in a rather dog-like way. I listened to the wind outside and checked the cat-flap. I had noticed earlier in the day that the lid of the rain barrel had been blown off. I put it back on again but maybe it had again been blown away and I was seized with a terrible and ridiculous fear that Susie had fallen in and then, suddenly, the cat-flap clicked and there she was. Wet and cross but alive and well.

The storm continued all the next day. I couldn't write. I sat at my desk and stared at the screen and there was a miasma of grief where there should have been images and ideas. The hours passed. I thought of ringing Miriam but she had no reception where she was and so it had to be the landline. I found her absence unbearable and did try ringing her once but there was just the infuriating BT answerphone and I didn't leave a message. Once again, Susie was not there for her supper. I had checked the rain barrel during the day and had tried to secure the lid, which was definitely loose, but I knew it would not hold. I am not practical. I listened to the monstrous gusts of wind and once again became gripped by the conviction that Susie had fallen in. Furious with Susie and furious with myself for my absurd fantasies I stormed out of the house, leaving the kitchen door open so that the light shone down the narrow paved path that led around the corner of the house to the barrel. The wind screeched through the tangled branches of the trees above me and I had to struggle to keep upright. The onset of the night's freeze was already apparent. Sure enough, when I got there the lid was gone but at that moment the wind blew the kitchen door shut and I could see very little. Pointlessly, I patted on the surface of the inky black water, my fingers freezing, squinting at it to make sure Susie was not there. And then suddenly she appeared from down the path and shot past me as a massive blast lifted the tops of the trees up and then bore down upon me and knocked me over. Falling, I grabbed at the rim of the barrel which fell on top of me, the weight of it pinning me to the ground as the ice-cold water flooded everywhere. My head hit the path hard. I lay there in the darkness, trying to breathe, water curling over and around me, frozen with shock and fear. The barrel was now lodged against the wall beside the path and the full weight of it was on me. I moved my head and a dreadful shaft of agony flew down my spine and into my pelvis. I began to cry. No-one would see me here. No-one would hear me and I was not even sure I had enough breath to call. I tried not to move to avoid that agonising spear of pain. My mind drifted. I shall die, I thought. Could I last the night? No. I couldn't. What would Miriam do when she rang and found no answer? Would she call a neighbour? Would anything be in time? My feet were numb and I realised that in falling I had trapped one arm behind my neck. It was suddenly agonising and yet I couldn't move it. I wondered if I was paralysed. I felt my chest trying and failing to cough out some of the water that had covered my face. I wished that I had lost consciousness and then I wondered whether I had. I had no way of knowing how long I had been there. There was no light and my watch was on my trapped arm. All I can remember was the soaring wind, the icy water and the creeping terror.

And then, a shaft of light. I looked up at the frantic movement of the branches overhead, their leaves glistening in the sudden glow from the kitchen door. A voice, Miriam's voice, shouting, calling, crying, and someone was rolling the barrel away, pulling at me, dragging me up the path. I may have blanked out for a bit for I next remember lying helplessly on our kitchen floor. Towels, warm towels, my dripping clothes tenderly removed, terrible pain. Blankets, duvets, pillows. I was sipping warm milk with, was it whisky? Miriam kneeling beside me, whimpering with fear and anxiety. Oh God. Oh God.

I have abandoned philosophy. And I have stopped trying to make sense of things. I didn't die that night but I had fractured my pelvis and dislocated my shoulder. And I was suffering from hypothermia. They kept me in hospital for almost a week. I had probably been unconscious for over an hour when Miriam found me and dragged me inside and called an ambulance. She had come back early because, she said, she had heard signs of distress in my voice the previous night. For months I was horribly disabled. We had to install a stairlift and I consider I aged ten years overnight. Sitting at a keyboard was impossible but that did not matter for I now found I had nothing to write. Certainly none of the usual stuff.

I had recognised that, on my way to death on that garden path, frozen and in agony, I was alone in a way I had never known before. I wanted time to think about that.

I am sitting today in the shade watching Miriam as she bustles about the garden in the early summer sunshine and I marvel at her energy and skill. The birds are busy about the feeders. I love her more than she knows; maybe more than even I know yet. I am new at this game but thanks to her I have a second chance. I might still die alone one day and she might die first and I know that and she knows that, and maybe that is the way it goes, but today we have this. We have talked about Ma Lindsey and her predictions and, since I am still without my keyboard skills, I am writing this longhand as Miriam has asked me to. She thinks it is a story that should be told. And then, maybe after some others, I plan to try my own *Mrs Dalloway*. I probably lack the talent but maybe I will find I am brave enough to attempt it after all.

ACKNOWLEDGEMENTS

Towards the end of 2017 I wrote a short story called 'Cat-Brushing' while on a two-week holiday with my eldest son, Nicholas, and his wife here in Bermuda. I used to brush Lucy, one of two ageing Siamese cats living here then. And as I was brushing Lucy, I caught sight of a dramatic black-and-white photograph on the kitchen dresser. It showed old, crabbed hands knitting; these were the hands of my daughter-in-law's much-loved grandmother. And so it was that into my head came a vision of an old woman who is brushing her cat while looking out through the kitchen door to watch the rain coming across the Great Sound. She is housebound and impoverished and now spends her days knitting, deprived by age of all the independence and health and respect she once enjoyed, fearing the loss of all she holds dear, including her only companion, the cat. Lucy arches her back with pleasure while she is brushed and the story gradually took shape in my mind.

Over the following four days, sitting at the kitchen table, I wrote the story, and then I sent it to the *London Review of Books*.

I am so grateful to the then Editor of the *LRB*, Mary-Kay Wilmers, who, despite not normally publishing fiction, wrote to me within a couple of weeks and published the story in the next edition. And it was Alice Spawls, the current Editor, who then encouraged me and introduced me to my agent Eleanor Birne at PEW Literary. Over the following years I wrote further stories and thanks to Eleanor's professional expertise and advice I have found my way to contracts with riverrun (Quercus) in the UK and Grove Atlantic in the US.

My most sincere thanks must go to Jon Riley and Jasmine Palmer at riverrun and Elisabeth Schmitz at Grove Atlantic for their skilful and patient editorial advice. I have profited from their guidance all the way.

I must also acknowledge my good fortune at this stage of my life in having a head still full of the words and images of Donne, de Maupassant, Keats, The Ancrene Riwle, Virgil, and Schopenhauer among others which now lie alongside theories basic to the practice of Group Analysis, my profession for the last thirty-five years. It is out of the amalgam of these disparate influences that the other twelve old women turned up in my mind, requiring that I write about them too.

Finally, throughout this process, I enjoyed the love and support of my four children, Fiona, Ruth, Nicholas and Alexander, without which these stories could not have been written.

BERMUDA, November 2021